MAKEUP OR BREAKUP?

Pam pointed out the Natural Shades Cosmetics model-search sign to her boyfriend, Jamal. "Doesn't it sound like fun? I'm sure I don't have a chance of winning, but—"

"You don't want to do this," Jamal said, interrupting her.

"Why not?" Pam asked.

"Because it's silly," Jamal replied. "Modeling? That stuff is for airheads." He glanced at her and shook his head. "Come on," he urged, taking her arm. "Let's get some dinner. I think you're getting faint with hunger. How else could you have such a ditzy idea?"

Pam felt her face burn with anger. How dare Jamal act as if what she did with her life was his decision? She yanked her arm from his grasp.

"You're wrong on both counts," Pam said firmly, her eyes flashing a warning. "First of all, I'm not hungry enough to eat dinner with *you* right now. And second, the Natural Shades Cosmetics search is *exactly* what I want to do."

NANCY DREW ON CAMPUS™

Available from ARCHWAY Paperbacks

Nancy Drew on campus™ #15

Loving and Losing

Carolyn Keene

AN ARCHWAY PAPERBACK
Published by POCKET BOOKS
New York London Toronto Sydney Tokyo Singapore

This book is a work of fiction. Names, characters, places and incidents are products of the author's imagination or are used fictitiously. Any resemblance to actual events or locales or persons, living or dead, is entirely coincidental.

AN ARCHWAY PAPERBACK *Original*

An Archway Paperback published by
POCKET BOOKS, a division of Simon & Schuster Inc.
1230 Avenue of the Americas, New York, NY 10020

Copyright © 1996 by Simon & Schuster Inc.
Produced by Mega-Books, Inc.

ISBN: 0-671-56804-3

First Archway Paperback printing November 1996

10 9 8 7 6 5 4 3 2 1

NANCY DREW, AN ARCHWAY PAPERBACK and colophon are registered trademarks of Simon & Schuster Inc.

NANCY DREW ON CAMPUS is a trademark of Simon & Schuster Inc.

Cover photos by Pat Hill Studio

Printed in the U.S.A.

IL 8+

CHAPTER 1

Bess Marvin leaned her cheek against the back of Paul Cody's warm fleece jacket and held him close, her arms snaking around his waist. She felt him lean to one side and moved with him instinctively as the motorcycle sped around a curve in the road. As they traveled to the top of a steep canyon in the state park near the Wilder University campus, they noticed that the road became narrower and rock walls jutted out at sharp angles to meet them.

Paul reached down and gave Bess's arm a quick squeeze. She shivered slightly at the touch of her boyfriend's fingers. He always makes me feel amazing, Bess thought.

The motorcycle slowed as they reached the top of the canyon. Paul pulled into a tiny parking area and switched off the engine. After they took off their helmets, Paul turned to Bess.

"I love to ride on this thing!" he exclaimed.

"Me, too," Bess said as they climbed off the bike. She felt exhilarated. "I'm so glad we came here," she said, shaking out her long golden hair.

"As long as I'm with you, I don't really care where we are," Paul replied, pulling Bess close and pressing his lips against hers.

"I love you," she murmured, holding him tight.

With their arms around each other, they stared at the incredible sight before them. The parking area overlooked a river valley. A waterfall spilled over the rim of a gorge directly across the canyon and crashed into the deep river pool below. Mist rose and turned to icy flakes in the cool air before settling back into the water.

"This is awesome. Nancy and Jake were right about this being the most beautiful view in all of Weston," Bess said.

When Bess had told her friends Nancy Drew and Jake Collins that she and Paul were planning a day in the country, they'd told her about the state park and this place overlooking the waterfall. Jake had once brought Nancy there for a romantic afternoon.

"This is great," Paul agreed. "But it's not the most beautiful sight in all of Weston."

"Oh, no?" Bess said softly. "And just what is?"

"You," he answered, staring into her light blue eyes.

Bess tilted her head so their lips could meet again. The taste of Paul's kisses and the warmth of being in his arms always made her heart pound.

She gently stroked Paul's left cheek. Bess noticed that it was as cold as her own. They had been out all day, and it was now late afternoon. With darkness approaching, the wind would feel even colder as they rode the motorcycle that they'd borrowed from Will Blackfeather, the boyfriend of Bess's cousin, George Fayne.

"We should think about getting back. Will and George might want to use the bike tonight."

Paul frowned. "Let's stay a little longer. I'm sure they won't mind if we get back later than we said. They'll understand two people having such an amazing day that they forgot all about time," Paul said as he nuzzled her neck.

Bess laughed and playfully tried to twist away from him. "It *has* been incredible," she said as he pulled her against his chest. "Our picnic at the meadow and the ride up here . . ."

"I only have eyes"—Paul kissed her ear—"and lips for you."

"Oh, Paul," Bess replied, as his warm breath fanned her cheek. "This is so perfect. I wish it didn't have to end."

"I hear a *but* coming," Paul moaned.

"But," Bess said with a chuckle, checking her

3

watch, "we really should go back to Wilder. It's getting colder, and—"

"I know, I know," Paul interrupted. He wrapped his arms around her. "You have to rehearse the one-acts."

"The performance is this Saturday!" Bess cried. "That's only two nights away. And I did say I'd meet Casey and Brian so we could rehearse tonight," Bess added, thinking of the promise she'd made to her friends and fellow actors, Casey Fontaine and Brian Daglian.

"I can't believe you're going to a rehearsal *and* to the Alpha Delt party tonight," Paul replied. "You *are* still planning to come to my frat party, aren't you?"

"Sure," Bess said. "I've been looking forward to it."

"You've got to stop worrying about the one-acts," Paul said, rubbing Bess's shoulders. "You're going to do great. These are just last-minute nerves. Besides, that acting coach already has her eye on you."

"I know," Bess replied. "But that just makes me more nervous. I really want to get into her class. Jeanne Glasseburg is going to be teaching here only next semester."

Bess knew that most of the invitations to the famous New York acting teacher's class would be extended to the upperclassmen in the theater department. But Glasseburg would also select a few drama students from the lower classes. She'd be at the opening-night performance of the one-act plays to see if there were any students in the production that she wanted in her class. That was why Bess's performance was so important—she was dying to get chosen for the class.

Bess thought she'd blown any chance of getting in when Jeanne Glasseburg happened to see her doing a spoof of the one-acts. Bess was sure she'd made a total fool of herself, but the truth was that Jeanne Glasseburg had loved Bess's improvisation.

"Why would you be more nervous if she already thinks you're talented?" Paul asked.

"If she hadn't seen the spoof, she probably wouldn't even have noticed me, but now she may expect something really good from me. I don't want to disappoint her," Bess said softly.

"She's not going to be disappointed, Bess," Paul replied.

"How can you be so sure?"

"Because she's not wrong," Paul said, grinning as he hugged Bess closer to him. "If you admire her so much, Bess, how can you doubt her judgment? She sees talent in you, so trust her. And trust yourself."

"You really believe in me, don't you?" Bess said.

"Of course I do," Paul answered. "And I'm also completely in love with you. But don't think that makes me biased."

Bess shivered again, but this time it wasn't

from nervousness. It was excitement—and happiness. She couldn't believe how fantastic her relationship with Paul was. Today had been really special.

Between schoolwork and Bess's rehearsals, they hadn't had much time for each other lately. And during the upcoming school break, they were both going home to see their parents, so it would be a while before they could be together like this again. Bess sighed.

"I know," Paul whispered. "I wish we could stay here forever, too."

"When did you start reading my mind?" Bess asked.

"Oh, the first minute we met." Paul laughed.

Bess snuggled closer to him. "We do need to head back soon," she said softly.

"In a minute," Paul replied, leaning toward her. "I really do love you, Bess." He ran a thumb along her cheekbone.

"I love you, too, Paul." Bess looked up into his eyes. "With all my heart."

Paul's lips captured hers, and Bess felt as if they would be together forever.

"All right, let's hear it," Nancy finally burst out, laughing at the expression on Dawn Steiger's face. "You look as if you might die if you don't talk to somebody."

"Hey, guys, what are you doing?" Casey Fontaine said as she walked into the lounge of Suite

301 in Thayer Hall where Nancy and Dawn, the resident adviser, were sitting.

"I'm waiting for Jake to pick me up to go to the Alpha Delt party, and Dawn here"—Nancy paused and pointedly turned to the beautiful blond girl sitting next to her on the couch—"is waiting to explode with some secret she's bottled up."

"Oooh, give it up," Casey cried. "If you have a secret, you'd better tell."

"Okay, okay. But it's not a secret. It's just about Bill." Dawn grinned, her pretty face flushing.

Bill Graham was the R.A. on the men's second floor in Thayer. Nancy thought he was a great guy, with a terrific sense of humor.

"I really like him," Dawn said.

"That's helpful," Casey replied, rolling her eyes at Nancy. "You two *have* been dating for a while now."

"Well," Dawn admitted, "we've been *friends* more than anything else. That was my choice."

"No kidding," Nancy said. "He's been head over heels in love with you for a long time."

"I know," Dawn agreed. "But I didn't think I could handle another relationship after my breakup with Peter," she added.

"Until now?" Casey said gleefully. "Good. It's finally love."

Dawn laughed. "I think so. Only now that I've admitted to myself how I feel, I want to spend some time alone with him and talk about how my feelings for him have deepened. And I want to really *show* him, if you know what I mean." Dawn smiled and blushed slightly. Then her smile faded. "But there's no way I can do that right now."

"Why not?" Casey asked.

"We can't find any time to be alone lately." Dawn sighed.

"But exams are over," Nancy said. "You'll have the whole weekend."

"That's what I thought," Dawn admitted. "I was looking forward to that. But Bill just told me that an old high school friend of his, Zach something-or-other, is coming up to Wilder—this weekend."

"Bad timing," Nancy murmured.

"I can't really be upset," Dawn said, "because Bill's so happy and excited about seeing Zach, who's been traveling around the world for the last year. Bill hasn't talked to him in ages."

Dawn sighed and absently pulled at a stray lock of blond hair. "Zach will arrive at Weston sometime tonight."

"They'll probably have lots to talk about," Nancy said.

"Which is okay." Dawn smiled. "I guess I'm looking forward to meeting such a good friend of Bill's."

Dawn looked at Nancy and Casey and frowned.

"But it means I have to wait a while before I get Bill all to myself.

"Oh, well," she said with a shrug, "I can't be selfish. I know he's really looking forward to Zach's visit."

"Sure he is," Casey agreed. "But I bet that on Monday, when you talk to him about *your* news, he won't remember who Zach is."

"It'll wipe every other thought from his mind," Nancy added.

"I hope," Dawn said softly. "I've always known what a wonderful guy Bill was. I've just been too afraid to let myself become vulnerable again."

Nancy knew exactly why Dawn was so nervous. The resident adviser had been really hurt and lost when her boyfriend, Peter, broke up with her. She'd even gotten involved for a while with REACH, a cult that preyed on lonely students like Dawn, drawing them in with false promises of friendship and then taking their money. Bill was the first to notice the change in Dawn's behavior. And together with Nancy, he had helped Dawn see the truth about REACH.

"You two will make a great couple," Nancy said.

"And we *always* like more romance in the dorm," Casey added.

"Poor Casey." Nancy laughed. "As if there's no romance in your life since you said yes to that gorgeous fiancé of yours."

"Allow me to live vicariously," Casey said. "Charley's in Los Angeles, and I get to see him once a month—if I'm lucky."

"It is wonderful to be falling in love again," Dawn admitted. "If only I get the chance to tell him soon."

Nancy didn't miss the impatience in Dawn's voice. It was great to see that Dawn was ready to listen to her heart and not just her head.

Nancy thought about her own fear of getting serious with another guy after breaking up with Ned Nickerson, her longtime boyfriend. But she'd followed her heart with Jake Collins, and she couldn't have been happier. Just thinking about him made her knees weak. The chemistry between them was electric.

Then, as if she'd summoned him, there was a knock on the suite door. When Nancy opened it, Jake stepped into the room. His brown hair was slightly tousled, making him look sexy, as usual. His eyes lit up when he saw Nancy. Jake started toward her, and Nancy knew he was going to take her in his arms.

In the distance she heard a phone ringing, and realized the sound was coming from her room.

"Is that your phone?" Jake asked, feigning anger. "It's ruining my entrance." He sighed as he plopped himself on the couch next to Casey.

"Sorry." Nancy grinned, wrinkling her nose at Jake. "Let me grab it. It won't take a sec. I'll be right back," she promised. Nancy jogged to her room and snatched up the phone.

"Hello?"

"Nancy? Is that you?"

Nancy recognized the voice of her Little Sister, Anna Pederson. Anna was twelve and lived in downtown Weston. Nancy had been matched up with Anna through Helping Hands, a Big Sister-Big Brother mentoring program on campus. Nancy usually spent a few hours a week with Anna, and they had a date to get together the next afternoon. But Nancy could hear how anxious Anna sounded on the phone.

"Anna?" Nancy asked worriedly. "Is something wrong?"

"No," Anna said quickly, sounding almost embarrassed. "I mean, yes. Nancy, I'm really worried about my dad."

"What is it?" Nancy asked, sitting down on her bed.

"Remember, I told you about my dad losing his job?" Anna said in a shaky voice. "Well, he went on another interview today, but he didn't get the job. He came home looking really mad."

"That's too bad," Nancy said. "But job-hunting is hard, and it can take a while to find a position. I'm sure he'll find one soon. Don't worry—"

"I have to worry!" Anna suddenly cried. "You don't understand." She sounded as if she might start crying. "He . . . my dad . . . he used to drink," Anna admitted softly, her voice choking.

11

"After my mom died. He hasn't in a long time, but he's been so upset lately. And now he's gone out, and he wouldn't tell me where he was going." Anna paused and Nancy heard her sniffling. "I'm afraid he might have started drinking again."

"Have you seen him drinking since he lost his job?" Nancy asked, her voice full of concern.

"No," Anna admitted. "But I'm really worried."

"I know," Nancy said. "But if he's stayed sober so far, I'm sure he'll be okay. He probably just needs to be alone for a while."

"I don't know . . ." Anna's voice trailed off.

"Listen," Nancy said gently. "Don't think about it anymore. Try to get some sleep. I'm sure your father will be fine, and you and I can talk about it when I pick you up tomorrow, okay?"

"Okay," Anna said, taking a deep breath. "Two o'clock, right?" she asked anxiously.

"Two o'clock," Nancy agreed. "Now get some sleep."

Nancy hung up the phone and walked back to the lounge, wishing she could do something more for Anna.

But I guess my being here for her to talk to is a big help, Nancy realized. Who else would Anna have called?

When Nancy saw Jake, she pushed away her concerns about Anna. She'd be able to spend time with Anna tomorrow. All she wanted now was to feel Jake's arms around her.

"Everything okay?" Jake asked as he pulled Nancy close to him.

"You bet," Nancy said, resting her cheek on his chest. "Now that you're here. But you've got to get me out of this suite," she added, shooting a glance at Dawn and Casey. "All these two want to talk about is love, love, love. It's so boring, don't you agree?" Nancy asked, turning her gaze on Jake.

"Oh, is it?" Jake grinned down at her. She knew he wanted to kiss her, but wouldn't in front of Casey and Dawn. Not the way he obviously wanted to.

"Later," he whispered, as though he'd read her mind. "I'll prove just how boring it *isn't*. I promise."

It was a promise Nancy was anxious to see fulfilled.

Bess hung on to Paul's waist as the motorcycle raced down the steep road. The bike picked up speed after they left the state park and entered the road leading back to Weston and the Wilder campus.

Bess and Paul had lingered by the waterfall longer than they should have. It was already dark when they climbed on the motorcycle for the long ride home. Bess knew they'd get back too late

13

for her to rehearse with Casey and Brian, but she'd see them at the party and apologize there.

It was incredible, but knowing she'd missed an opportunity to rehearse didn't bother Bess. In fact, she wasn't feeling at all nervous now about her upcoming performance. Paul's supportive words had really made an impression on her.

Bess couldn't wait for Saturday night. Jeanne Glasseburg's class was within reach, and Bess was sure she would be chosen for it.

It felt so good to have a boyfriend who believed in her the way Paul did. This is what love is all about, Bess thought, hugging Paul tighter.

"I love you," Bess cried, leaning forward so her voice wouldn't be drowned out by the whine of the engine and the whistling air.

"What?" Paul yelled back.

Bess felt the question more than she actually heard it, as though the minute Paul spoke the word was already fifty feet behind them.

Bess shook her head and squeezed him to let him know it was nothing. She could tell him when they were back at Wilder, and she'd thank him again for making her feel so confident. Suddenly Bess had an incredible rush of feeling, and she knew, just knew, that she and Paul would be together for a long time. Maybe even—

Before Bess could finish the thought, she was blinded by a flash of light and automatically tightened her grip around Paul's waist.

She heard the sound of screeching tires, and

then something hit the back of the motorcycle. The machine spun and skidded. Bess lost her hold on Paul, and she screamed as she flew off the motorcycle. The dark shadows of the trees flew past her sideways, and for a second Bess saw her own feet against the stars.

She'd lost Paul—her hands were grasping air. Then all at once she hit the ground—and everything went black.

CHAPTER 2

Pam Miller stepped out of the library and burrowed her chin deep into her scarf as a cold wind blew across the Wilder campus. Now that it was dark, the air was a lot colder than it had been when she left her dorm that morning. Pam hunched her shoulders and walked down the path to the African-American Cultural Alliance Center, where she was to meet her boyfriend, Jamal Lewis, before going out for dinner.

She and Jamal had been dating for years and had gone through most of high school as boyfriend and girlfriend. Jamal was a year older than Pam and had always looked out for her in a protective way.

Back in high school Pam had thought his protectiveness was really sweet. He did things for her, like making sure she had a warm enough coat and seeing that she studied hard for a test or bought the best running shoes.

But now that they were both in college, Jamal was still trying to take care of her and run her life, and Pam didn't like it. Just tonight, when Jamal had found her in the library, he'd arranged the rest of her evening without even asking for her opinion.

"Meet me at seven at the alliance center," Jamal had said, bending down to kiss her neck. "We'll go out for dinner, and then we'll meet Trudy at Java Joe's for coffee."

Pam had been reading a really interesting article she'd found in the microfiche files while looking for ideas for a political theory paper she had to write. Jamal wanted to meet in half an hour, and Pam knew she wouldn't be able to finish reading the article. She'd tried to change their plans, but Jamal had said no.

"Trust me," he had said. "You need to eat. Take a break. What's more important, an article or me?"

Before she could answer, he was gone.

Pam knew Jamal loved her, and she didn't want to hurt him, but he wasn't simply looking out for her anymore. Too much of the time he was telling her what to do, and Pam was beginning to resent it.

"I can think for myself, after all," Pam muttered as she pushed open the door of the AACA

Center and stepped into the lobby. Pam checked her watch and saw that she had a few minutes before Jamal would arrive.

As she passed the bulletin board, a large, brightly colored poster caught her eye, and Pam paused to read it.

Youth and Beauty—Naturally!
Natural Shades Cosmetics Needs You
for a New Natural Shades for Youth Campaign.

Pam knew all about Natural Shades Cosmetics. It was a successful Chicago-based company whose products were designed for African-American women. She sold the products at Berrigan's cosmetics counter where she worked part-time, and Pam even used them herself. Quickly she scanned the rest of the notice.

Natural Shades was launching a new line of cosmetics for women in their teens and twenties. They were searching for three college students—one from the East Coast, one from the West Coast, and one from the Midwest—whose faces would be featured in their new ad campaign.

The notice said that representatives of the company were visiting midwestern schools and would be at Wilder tomorrow!

An image of her face on the cover of a magazine floated before Pam's eyes. She chuckled in embarrassment and checked to see if anyone had noticed.

Pam traced the date on the notice with her finger. She was definitely tempted. It would be incredibly glamorous and exciting to see her face in an ad, not to mention how great the money would be. She'd never seriously considered modeling before. But why not? Pam thought. I'm smart, but that doesn't mean I can't be beautiful, too.

"Hey, gorgeous!" a voice spoke in her ear. Pam jumped and spun around. It was Jamal, a big grin spread across his dark handsome face.

"You startled me," Pam said, turning back to the poster.

"I should have known you'd have your eyes stuck to some bulletin board," Jamal joked, standing behind her. "What are you checking out? Sports tryouts? Political rally?"

"No," Pam answered. "Look, this is something really exciting." She pointed at the notice and then turned around to grab Jamal's arm. "Doesn't it sound like fun? I'm sure I don't have a chance of winning, but—"

"You don't want to do this," Jamal said, interrupting her.

"Why not?" Pam asked.

"Because it's silly," Jamal replied. "Modeling? Come on, Pam. That stuff is for airheads. You don't care about makeup. Not like that, I mean."

"Like what?" Pam pressed. "What's wrong with looking pretty?"

"You're more than just a pretty face," Jamal

19

replied. "Modeling isn't for you." He glanced at her and shook his head. "Come on," he urged, taking her arm. "Let's get some dinner. I think you're getting faint with hunger. How else could you have such a ditzy idea?"

Pam felt her face burn with anger. How dare Jamal act as if what she did with her life was his decision? She was tired of this. She yanked her arm from his grasp.

"You're wrong on both counts," Pam said firmly, her eyes flashing a warning. "First of all, I'm not hungry enough to eat dinner with *you* right now. And second, the Natural Shades Cosmetics search is *exactly* what I want to do."

Stephanie Keats was dying for a cigarette, but that was the only thing dampening her good mood when she returned to Thayer Hall that night. That afternoon her shift at Berrigan's had seemed to fly by after Jonathan Bauer, the gorgeous floor manager whom Stephanie was crazy about, had asked her to have dinner with him after work.

They'd gone to the Rose Café, right next to Berrigan's. It was low-key and homey, and mostly a hangout for Weston locals—the sort of place Stephanie usually wouldn't have been caught dead in. But she was surprised at how much she'd enjoyed eating there. Stephanie'd had a great evening, even though Jonathan hadn't flirted with her at all. They'd spent the whole time talking, which was something Stephanie hadn't done with a handsome guy in a very long time, if ever.

Jonathan hadn't actually said anything about smoking, but Stephanie knew he didn't approve, so she wasn't comfortable smoking in front of him. Somehow that made her very uncomfortable, having to admit to herself that she didn't want to disappoint a man.

Stephanie couldn't hold off a nicotine fit any longer, and she fished in her bag for her cigarettes as she stood outside Thayer Hall.

It's not as though I'm going to change my life for him or anything, Stephanie reminded herself, pulling a cigarette out of her crumpled pack and lifting it to her lips.

But before she could find a lighter, the flame of a match appeared out of nowhere. Calmly Stephanie bent to touch the tip of her cigarette to the flame. As she breathed in, she let her eyes trail from the match to the strong tan fingers that held it, then up past incredibly broad shoulders, to an amazingly gorgeous face framed by sun-streaked dark hair.

Stephanie's eyes darted away as she exhaled slowly.

Mr. Gorgeous blew out the match and tossed it into a nearby litter basket.

"I'm Zach." He smiled, flashing straight white teeth. "Zach Bainbridge."

"Stephanie Keats," Stephanie replied, her voice automatically dropping a note.

"I'm pleased to meet you, Stephanie," Zach continued, his eyes showing his interest. "I hope I can be of service again." He nodded at her lit cigarette. "Any kind of service at all," he added mischievously.

Whoever this guy Zach was, he was a major flirt. Stephanie stared back at him coolly. And incredibly good-looking, she added to herself.

"I'll keep that in mind," Stephanie replied. "I do appreciate a well-trained man."

"And I appreciate a well-shaped woman," Zach said smoothly, his gaze traveling the length of her body. "The pleasure is mine. I hope."

It had been a while since any guy had come on to Stephanie so forcefully, and she had to admit she was enjoying it.

Then an image of Jonathan floated into her mind: The way he listened so intently to her when she spoke, as though he really cared about what she was saying. Stephanie pulled her eyes away from Zach's determined gaze. Thinking about Jonathan was confusing her.

She saw a large duffel bag resting by Zach's feet. It was decorated with patches from countries all over the world. Australia, China, Spain—just a few of the places Zach's bag advertised.

"I see you get around, Mr. Bainbridge," Stephanie commented, determined to keep the conversation going but not really knowing why.

"I've been a place or two," Zach admitted. "In fact, I'd love to tell you about it. Traveling can get so lonely," he said, raising an eyebrow at her. "It's nice to find someone to share with."

Stephanie was about to cut off their conversation, when she stopped herself. Why shouldn't she hang out with Zach? It wasn't as though she and Jonathan were serious. What harm was there in talking to another guy?

"Well," Zach pressed, leaning a little closer. "Am I going to get you? For an audience, I mean?"

She wasn't interested in Zach romantically, Stephanie reminded herself. But whether she was interested or not, Zach was gorgeous and intriguing and he was clearly interested in her.

No harm in playing along, Stephanie decided, grinning flirtatiously.

"Only if you're stimulating," Stephanie said slyly. "I wouldn't want to fall asleep on you."

"Oh, I'll keep you awake." Zach chuckled. "I promise."

"Who's that girl with Dennis?" Nancy asked Jake, pointing to the door of the Alpha Delt house as one of Jake's roommates, Dennis Larkin, arrived.

"I don't know." Jake shrugged and stood on tiptoe, waving his arms and yelling, "Hey, Dennis!" across the crowd. Dennis spotted them and started over.

Standing next to Nancy were George Fayne and her boyfriend, Will Blackfeather. "She's beautiful," George said, raising her hand to shield Will's eyes. "Don't look," George warned. "You'll turn to salt. I hope."

"Hey, guys." Dennis grinned, his straight white teeth flashing in his dark face.

"It's nice to see you out," Jake commented dryly. "I was starting to worry about you."

"It's good to have a reason to come out," Dennis joked. "This is my friend Tamara," he said, introducing the elegantly beautiful girl next to him. She was one of the most exotic-looking women Nancy had ever seen, with her long dark hair, green eyes, and milk-chocolate skin.

"I just *love* Thursday-night parties," Tamara said. "It makes the weekend seem so much longer."

"Except for the sad few of us who actually have Friday classes," Dennis moaned.

"You've got to learn to schedule your hours better," George replied.

"True," Dennis agreed. "I knew a guy who had all his classes on Tuesday and Wednesday. He had a five-day weekend, and believe me, he took advantage of it. For three years."

"Yeah, I remember that guy," Jake added. "He was definitely a party animal."

"He sounds pretty clever," Nancy said. "I'd like to have a schedule like that someday."

"I don't know what I'd do with all my time," George replied. "I'd hardly feel like I was in school."

"You'd spend it with me, of course," Will replied easily. Nancy watched as Will pulled

George into his arms. "Just like you will when we get our long weekend," Will added.

Nancy felt an arm slip around her waist and grinned up at Jake.

"That's right," Jake said. "It's going to be the attack of the Wilder boyfriends on River Heights. You're still looking forward to it, aren't you, Drew?"

Nancy smiled. She'd decided to invite Jake home with her over the short break coming up. George had also invited Will to her home, and Nancy was sure the four of them would have a great time together.

Nancy had been a little nervous about bringing Jake to her hometown, since so many memories there were of her and Ned. But she really wanted to share some of her past with Jake, and have him meet her family.

"Of course I'm excited," Nancy replied meaningfully, raising her arm to circle his neck. Her bare arm tingled where it rested across his warm neck. Nancy stood on tiptoe and brushed her cheek against his. It was soft and smooth. Nancy took a little sniff and grinned. She loved the way Jake smelled after a shave.

"What about you?" she whispered into his ear. "Having any second thoughts?"

Nancy felt Jake's arm tighten around her waist, and she chuckled. She loved to tease him like this, because it was so much fun.

"Only about being here," Jake growled softly.

"I'd give up a good lead article to make everyone around us disappear right now."

"Nancy!" a voice called out, interrupting her thoughts.

Nancy pulled away from Jake to see Liz Bader, one of her suitemates, pushing toward them through the crowd on the dance floor.

Nancy saw that Liz's delicate features were pinched in concern. Daniel Frederick, an Alpha Delt member and Liz's boyfriend, was right behind her, and he appeared to be just as upset.

"Nancy, I'm so glad we found you!" Liz cried, when she and Daniel finally reached the group. "You have an urgent call."

"Sorry to interrupt your fun," Daniel added apologetically. "A girl named Leslie is on the phone. She wants to talk to you right away."

"Leslie?" Nancy asked, surprised. Leslie King was Bess's roommate.

"She asked for you or George," Liz replied quickly. "Whoever we could find first."

"She said it was an emergency," Daniel explained. "I've got her on the line in another room."

Nancy turned and caught George's eye. "Something's happened to Bess?" George asked worriedly.

"Where's the phone?" Nancy replied.

"Follow me." Daniel turned and snaked his way back through the crowd. Nancy and George were right behind him with Jake, Will, and Liz bringing up the rear. They pushed their way into a small library off the main room.

Nancy hurried to the phone and snatched up the handset.

"Leslie?" she asked, hoping the other girl hadn't given up waiting.

"Nancy! Is that you?" Leslie asked, her voice thick with relief. "It's about Bess. Nancy, she's in the county hospital."

Nancy inhaled sharply. "In the hospital?" she repeated. Instantly George was beside her.

"The staff found her Wilder ID and called the university," Leslie said. "I'm so glad I was in our room. They've already called her parents—"

"Leslie, what happened?" Nancy interrupted.

"She and Paul had an accident on the motorcycle," Leslie explained.

"How is she?" Nancy asked quickly. George's fingers were digging into Nancy's arm.

"I don't know!" Leslie cried over the phone. Nancy could hear Leslie trying hard to keep her emotions in check. "They told me she was still being examined."

"What about Paul?" Nancy asked.

"I asked about him, too," Leslie said, "but the nurse wouldn't tell me anything."

"Okay, Leslie," Nancy said, checking her watch. "We're leaving right now. We'll be at the hospital in ten minutes."

"Oh, Nancy," Leslie said, starting to cry, "I'm afraid it's bad. Really, really bad."

CHAPTER 3

George almost knocked a nurse over as she raced into the emergency room of the Weston County Hospital. She'd barely been able to sit still for the ten-minute car ride, and she knew she had probably cut off the circulation in Will's fingers, she'd been gripping them so tightly. As Nancy pulled her Mustang in between two ambulances, George bolted from the car without waiting for it to stop. Will, Nancy, and Jake were right behind her.

"My cousin is here—Bess Marvin," George said to the nurse at the admissions desk. "She was in a motorcycle accident."

"Oh, yes." The nurse nodded, coming around the desk and leading George and the others out of the waiting room and into the emergency wing.

A gray-haired doctor in a long white coat came toward them.

"Dr. Levy," the nurse explained, "these are relatives of the woman who was in the motorcycle accident."

"She's my cousin," George said quickly. "My name is George Fayne."

"I'm Dr. Levy," he replied.

"How is Bess?" George asked shakily.

"Your cousin has suffered a concussion and a broken arm," Dr. Levy began. "Four of her ribs are bruised, though luckily they're not broken, and she sustained numerous cuts and scrapes. She's been badly banged up," the doctor continued. "But we've checked her out thoroughly, and there appear to be no life-threatening injuries."

The relief was so strong, George knew she would have collapsed if Will's arms hadn't been around her.

"She'll have to stay here for a few days," Dr. Levy continued. "And after that, she'll still need a number of weeks to recover fully."

"But she will recover?" George asked.

"I think she'll be fine." Dr. Levy smiled. "With rest. We've gotten in touch with her parents," he added.

"Dr. Levy," Will said, "what about the guy she was riding with?"

George looked up at Will quickly. His mouth was set in a tight line as he waited for the doctor's reply.

"That's right!" Nancy exclaimed. "Was Paul injured?"

"I *know* he was wearing a helmet," Will said.

"That's true," the doctor replied slowly. "He was."

Dr. Levy paused, and George felt prickles of fear in her stomach. She could see that all her friends were holding their breath.

Dr. Levy dropped his gaze to the floor and cleared his throat. "I'm sorry to have to tell you this," he began, "but there was nothing we could do for him. Your friend was already dead when the ambulance brought him in."

George felt a wave of dizziness wash over her. Instinctively, she reached out and grabbed Will's shirt, but he was hardly steady himself.

"We did all we could," Dr. Levy explained, "but it was just too late. And given the extent of his injuries, I don't know if we could have saved him even if EMS had gotten to him sooner."

George knew that only one part of her brain was taking in the information as the doctor kept speaking. With the other part she was trying to convince herself that she wasn't hearing what the doctor had just told her.

You must have misunderstood, a voice was saying. Or they've made a mistake. Paul can't be dead."

"That can't be true," George whispered, knowing as she spoke that it was.

Paul Cody was dead.

George looked over at Nancy and Jake. Nancy was still shaking her head in disbelief. Jake was behind her, holding on to both of her arms, his face pale.

"Does Bess know?" George asked. She turned to Dr. Levy. "Has she been told that Paul is—" George couldn't finish. She just couldn't say it. Not yet.

"Bess was unconscious when EMS arrived at the scene," Dr. Levy replied. "She was still out when she was brought in. She's stabilized now," he continued. "But, no, she hasn't been told."

George glanced over at Nancy, the expression on her face a silent question. Nancy nodded back.

"We have to see her," George said shakily.

We'll make sure she's okay, George thought. And then would come the hard part. Perhaps the most difficult thing George would ever do. She would have to tell Bess about Paul.

"Spider and Denny have been gone forever," Ray Johansson complained, pacing the big garage that served as the rehearsal space for his band, the Beat Poets. "We can't afford to waste time like this. And where in the world are Sam and Bruce? They were supposed to be here a half hour ago!"

Ginny Yuen frowned as she watched her boyfriend stalk around the room. Denny, Spider, Sam, and Bruce were the members of the band, and the group had planned on an all-night jam session. Denny and Spider were out buying snacks, and they hadn't been gone more than ten minutes. But Ray had been practically climbing the walls since they left.

"This record deal is the most important thing that's ever happened to us," Ray was saying. "It's our one chance. We just can't blow it."

The Beat Poets had a signed a contract with Pacific Records, a huge company out in California, and soon they would be recording their first CD.

"You won't blow it," Ginny assured him.

"I don't know. School is really becoming a drag," Ray admitted, running a hand through his short jet-black hair. "We've got a killer schedule if we're going to be ready for the recording session. I hardly have time for the band, let alone homework. I don't even know why I'm still trying," Ray said under his breath.

Ginny winced. Ray was thinking of dropping out of school and moving to L.A. so he'd be able to practice and work on his music full-time. She had to bite her tongue to keep from saying something. She was worried that if she tried to persuade Ray not to quit school, it would just feel like more pressure. And she knew he had to make the decision on his own.

But Ginny didn't want him to go. First, because quitting school seemed like such a huge step. She felt guilty for thinking it, but what if the Beat

Poets didn't take off? Then what? Ray would have thrown away his education.

Of course, the main reason she didn't want Ray to leave was selfish. What would happen to their relationship if Ray moved to L.A.? Ginny forced the question from her mind, as she'd done so often during the last few weeks.

"Don't worry, you'll get everything done." Ginny said, trying to make him feel better.

"Easy for you to say," Ray muttered. "You're a genius. I'm pretty sure I failed my last exam. And I've got a monster paper due on Monday." He shook his head. "It's probably a lost cause already."

Ginny could see that Ray was really on edge, but she needed to talk to him about something besides the Pacific Records deal. She had worries of her own.

"My volunteer work at the hospital starts tomorrow," Ginny finally blurted out. "It's part of the premed program."

"Mm-hmm," Ray muttered, bending down to fiddle with one of the wires for his guitar amplifier.

"The job's supposed to be really good," she added.

"Why do it if you're thinking about not going to med school?" Ray answered sharply, frowning at the amplifier's readout. "This thing is shot," he muttered, kicking the small amplifier with his boot. "Hold on a sec," he added, stalking across the room. He flipped open a cardboard box and started pulling out a mass of tangled wires and cables.

Ginny sighed. So much for Ray's opinion.

She had come to Wilder planning to be a doctor, which was what her parents had always wanted and expected from her. But since she'd met Ray, Ginny was doing lots of things she'd never thought she would do, such as dating the lead singer of a rock band and writing lyrics for some of Ray's music.

This newfound creativity was making Ginny question whether she wanted to be a doctor or not. She just didn't know what she wanted to do.

Except actually *talk* to Ray about it all, she thought, watching his tense face.

"I'm not sure I won't be going to med school," Ginny finally said.

"What?" Ray asked, lifting his eyes. "But you're not. Didn't you already say that."

"No, I just said I wasn't sure—" Ginny began.

The door at the side of the garage slammed open and Spider and Denny staggered in, their arms full of brown paper bags stuffed with chips and soda.

"It's about time," Ray said. "Come on, guys." He picked up his guitar. "I'm not waiting any longer for Sam and Bruce. We need to rehearse if we're going to be ready for this recording session. We can work on some riffs without them."

Ginny moved back and plopped herself down

on the battered couch, her chin in her hands. She loved Ray, but she was getting a little tired of taking a backseat to his record deal. She couldn't remember the last time they'd had a serious conversation, especially about their relationship.

"She should still be awake," Dr. Levy explained in a soft voice, standing in front of a white curtain in the emergency room. George and Nancy stood beside him, waiting nervously. "But we've just given her some heavy painkillers. They'll knock her out soon, which will be for the best. In a few hours we'll move her to a private room."

Dr. Levy pushed aside the curtain and stepped back. Beside her, George heard Nancy's sharp intake of breath.

"It hardly looks like Bess," Nancy whispered. "Bess is so lively, full of energy . . ."

George couldn't reply. She was too stunned. Nancy was right. George wouldn't have believed it was Bess in that bed if she hadn't been told.

One of Bess's arms was in a cast. She looked so tiny and vulnerable lying in the middle of the blinding white room, tethered by tubes to a huge black machine blinking away in the corner. George watched Bess's heartbeat cross the screen in regular rhythms and finally released the breath she'd been holding.

George stepped forward tentatively.

"Bess?" she said softly, moving to the bed.

George could see an enormous purple bruise ballooning on Bess's right cheek and a big cut on her forehead. George could see that the cut had only needed a few stitches, so it probably wouldn't leave a scar.

Bess's eyes fluttered open a few times. Finally she kept them open and focused on George.

George tried to smile. "Bess," she said softly, "you're going to be okay."

But Bess just shook her head.

"We spoke to the doctor," George added, bending down over her cousin. "He said you have no serious injuries. You're mostly just banged up. You're going to be fine."

"No," Bess murmured, still shaking her head.

"What is it?" George asked, wondering if Bess was in too much pain to hear them. "Bess?"

"Paul," Bess whispered. "What about Paul?"

"Shhh," George replied softly, stroking Bess's hand, trying to avoid her question.

I can't tell her, George thought worriedly. Not right now. It'll be too much.

"Paul," Bess croaked. "Please, I want to see Paul. He's okay, isn't he?"

George turned helplessly to Nancy, who nodded, her eyes filling with tears.

"Oh, Bess," George whispered. "Bess, I'm so sorry." George gulped back her emotions.

"George?" Bess moaned, her eyes pleading. "George, tell me about Paul. They won't tell me if he's okay, they won't—"

"He didn't make it," George choked out. "Bess . . . Paul is dead."

Bess's mouth opened. She started gulping in air and struggling to sit up.

"Bess, we're so sorry," Nancy said, leaning over her on the other side of the bed.

"Please," George said, holding Bess down as gently as she could. "There's nothing you can do."

"Paul," Bess whimpered. "But I had to tell him . . . He has to be there. . . . George, he has to be."

Tears were streaming down Bess's cheeks, and George carefully wiped them away. She watched with relief as Bess's pupils dilated and her eyelids began to close.

"The drugs are kicking in," Nancy whispered.

"Don't think any more now," George said as Bess's head fell back on to the pillows. It will be hard enough later, she thought, imagining what Bess would have to face when she awoke.

George felt her heart break for her cousin as she and Nancy quietly left the room. Bess had lost the man she loved, and George knew it would take a long, long time for Bess to heal.

"The motorcycle is a wreck," the police officer said as he stood with Will and Jake in the emergency waiting room. "Did it belong to the kid driving?"

"No," Will admitted, feeling a stab of guilt. "It

was mine. I lent it to him this afternoon. I can't believe they had an accident."

"The girl couldn't tell us much when we got to the scene of the accident," the officer said. "She was pretty messed up. Luckily she was thrown to the side of the road," he continued. "The EMS guys said that's what saved her, landing on the grass."

Will's eyes widened. He hadn't thought just how lucky Bess was. He could barely believe that Paul was dead. Will couldn't imagine what he would have felt like if both of them . . . He didn't finish the thought.

"The guy was unlucky," the officer said. "He hit the concrete highway at more than fifty miles an hour."

Jake winced. "And his helmet didn't help?" he asked, disturbed.

"It protected his head," the officer replied. "But he suffered massive internal injuries and broken bones. He'd already lost too much blood by the time EMS arrived. He died before they got him back here."

The officer fell silent as George and Nancy came into the waiting room. Will could see the dark shadows under George's eyes. He held his arms open, and George ran to him and leaned heavily against his chest.

"How is Bess?" he asked softly. George just shook her head and sighed.

"She wanted to know about Paul," George replied sadly.

Will felt another stab of guilt. He was glad that neither Nancy nor George had heard the description of Paul's injuries. Or how close Bess had come to the same fate.

"Does anyone know what happened?" Will asked the police officer as he was ready to leave. "I mean, whose fault it was?"

Will had let Paul take the motorcycle because he trusted Paul's ability to drive. But maybe that had been a mistake. It had been a while since Paul had been on a motorcycle.

"It wasn't your friend's fault, if that's what you want to know," the man replied. "A car sped out of a side road. A witness said the kids on the motorcycle had no chance to get out of its way."

"There was a witness?" Jake asked.

The officer nodded. "That's who reported the accident. The witness said the driver ran a stop sign and clipped the back wheel of the bike. The kid driving the motorcycle lost control."

"And what happened to the driver of the car?" Nancy asked.

"We don't know," the man answered, shaking his head. "Apparently the driver took off."

"So it was a hit-and-run," Nancy said, anger coloring her words.

"Exactly," the police officer said. "But the witness gave us a good description of the car and a partial plate number. I'm almost positive we'll be able to track down the driver, especially if it's a local person."

Will was following the conversation, but he didn't have anything else to ask. He'd heard all he needed to: the driver of the bike had lost control.

The words rang in Will's head.

Did that mean a more experienced rider would have been able to avoid such a serious accident? Will wondered. Had the other car really hit the motorcycle that hard?

Will couldn't know the answers, and anyway it was too late for them to matter. The one thing he knew for sure was that he had played a part in the tragedy.

If only he hadn't let Bess and Paul take the motorcycle, Will thought, everyone would have been fine. He and his friends wouldn't be at the hospital. And Paul would still be alive.

CHAPTER 4

By the time Nancy pulled herself out of bed the next morning, everyone in the suite was up. As she walked into the lounge, Nancy could see from the red-rimmed eyes of Casey, Stephanie, Ginny Yuen, Reva Ross, Kara Verbeck, and Liz Bader that they had already heard about the accident and Paul's death.

But her suitemates wanted to hear it from her, so Nancy quickly recounted the scene in the hospital the night before. When she finished relating how she and George had told Bess about Paul, there wasn't a dry eye in the suite.

"It doesn't seem possible," Casey said, wiping her cheeks. "I saw Bess yesterday morning before she left with Paul. We were going to rehearse together last night, but Bess never called.

41

Brian and I figured she was hanging out with Paul somewhere, getting all lovey-dovey—" Casey fell silent and shook her head.

There was a knock on the suite door. Dawn got up to answer it, and Bill Graham stepped into the lounge, followed by a gorgeous guy Nancy had never seen before.

Must be Bill's friend, Nancy realized. She noticed that his eyes went right to Stephanie and lit up with recognition.

"Stephanie," the guy murmured silkily. "It's great to see you again."

Stephanie nodded back, arching her brow at the curious looks from her suitemates. Nancy wasn't surprised that Stephanie had managed to meet a handsome guy before anyone else.

"You've already met someone in this suite?" Bill asked. He punched his friend in the arm. "Still an operator," he said, then turned to Dawn.

"I hope I'm not interrupting," Bill said. "I wanted to introduce you to the friend I told you about. Zach Bainbridge, Dawn Steiger."

Nancy couldn't help noticing the appreciative look Zach gave Dawn as he took her hand. He even bowed his head. Bill wasn't kidding, Nancy realized. Zach really was an operator when it came to good-looking women.

"It's nice to meet you, Zach," Dawn said, her voice subdued.

Immediately Bill picked up on her mood. He

took a second look around the roomful of women and noticed the drawn expressions on their faces.

"Looks like we interrupted something serious," Bill said, concerned. "Is anything wrong?"

"I guess you haven't heard," Nancy said.

"There was an accident last night," Dawn added. "Bess Marvin and Paul Cody were riding a motorcycle back to campus. There was a hit-and-run accident. Bess was hurt pretty badly," Dawn paused. "And Paul was killed."

"Oh, no," Bill said. He turned toward Nancy, a stricken expression on his face. "Not Paul," Bill said, shaking his head. "He's such a great guy. And Bess?"

"She'll be okay," Nancy replied. "But it'll take time."

"Someone was killed?" Zach echoed, startled. "Wow."

"Sorry for barging in like this," Bill said softly. "I wish I knew what to say."

"It's okay," Dawn said quickly, reaching out to squeeze his arm. Bill put his arm around her shoulders.

"You said it was a hit-and-run," Bill said. "Do the police have any leads on the driver who hit them?"

"Not yet," Nancy admitted. "They hope to track down the car, but we'll just have to wait and see. A witness gave them a description of the car and part of a plate number."

"There was a witness?" Zach asked.

Nancy nodded.

Zach shook his head. "The accident must have been an awful thing to see."

"I'm sure it was," Nancy replied. "But it's lucky someone witnessed it and could give the police so much information about the car."

"Yeah," Zach said softly.

"I just got off the phone with Emmet," Eileen O'Connor said, stepping into the lounge. Emmet Lehman was Eileen's boyfriend. He lived at Zeta house and had been Paul's roommate. "He picked up Paul's parents at the airport this morning."

"I wonder how they're holding up," Nancy said softly. "It must be terrible for them."

"Can you imagine getting a call like that in the middle of the night?" Kara asked, her eyes full of sympathy.

"I can't imagine getting a call like that, ever," Reva whispered.

"They're going to take Paul—his body—back to Ohio for the funeral," Eileen added. "As soon as they can get permission, I guess."

"Ohio?" Dawn asked. "I wonder if any of his friends here will be able to go? Maybe we can organize a bus or something." She turned to Bill. "Would the university do that?"

"I don't know if the university is doing anything," Eileen offered. "But Emmet told me that the Zetas are planning a candlelight vigil for Paul down at the lake tonight, so that those who can't make it to the funeral can at least get together to remember him."

"That's a beautiful thing to do," Ginny commented.

"What a totally depressing way to spend a Friday night," Stephanie said. "But I'll be there."

"Me, too," Kara and Liz said together. The rest of the girls nodded their agreement.

Eileen checked her watch. "I have to run. I'm on my way to meet Emmet. I know being with Paul's parents has been draining on him, not to mention his own loss. He told me he really needs to go sit somewhere quiet for a while."

"He's lucky to have you to turn to." Dawn smiled.

"I guess," Eileen replied sadly.

"I'm going to call Brian and Chris," Casey said. "I want to make sure they've heard the news. I know Brian will want to go see Bess."

As the room emptied, Nancy remembered the call she'd been thinking of making ever since she heard the news of the accident.

She knew that her ex-boyfriend, Ned Nickerson, would want to know about Bess. During the time that he and Nancy were dating, they'd spent as much time with Bess and George as they had alone.

It had been a long time since she'd spoken to Ned, Nancy realized as she walked back to her room. Just as she reached for the phone, though, it rang. She was so startled, it took a second for her to catch her breath. She picked up the receiver.

"Hello?"

"Nancy, it's me, Anna," a sobbing voice came over the line. "I need your help."

"Anna, what's wrong?" Nancy asked.

"The police have my dad," Anna managed to say, her voice catching in her throat, "and I don't know what to do!"

"What are you talking about?" Nancy asked. "Slow down and tell me what's happened."

"My father's in jail," Anna said. "He never came home—"

"Anna, try to relax," Nancy said slowly, trying to calm her, "I can't help unless you explain it to me. What do you mean he never came home?"

"I told you!" Anna sobbed. "I knew something bad would happen. I was worried about him, but you said everything would be okay. But it's *not* okay. There was a car accident!"

"Is your father hurt?" Nancy asked worriedly. Maybe Mr. Pederson had gone drinking, she thought, feeling a twinge of guilt for the way she'd brushed off Anna's fears the day before. Nancy would feel awful if he'd actually hurt himself.

"No," Anna said. "It was someone else. There was a hit-and-run accident, and someone died, Nancy! And the police put my dad in jail because they say he did it. I was at the market this morning, and the cops came to the house while I was gone, and they took my dad," Anna sobbed.

"He called me to tell me where he was," she continued. "He says he didn't do it, and I know he didn't. But now he's in jail!"

Nancy went numb. Was Anna talking about the accident Bess and Paul had been in? Could such a terrible coincidence have occurred? Was Mr. Pederson the one who had hit them? Who had killed Paul?

"Nancy!" Anna sobbed, interrupting her thoughts. "Please, I don't have anyone else to call. I need your help!"

When Bess woke, she groggily focused on the white walls and curtains. She felt aches and pains shooting all through her body. Where was she?

She blinked, and all at once memories of the night before came rushing back.

Paul was dead.

Bess started to cry. She thought about how wonderful the day had been before . . . before . . .

A picnic in the chilly autumn air. The beautiful ride through the countryside. The waterfall. Paul's warm lips on hers. They'd lingered for long time, Bess recalled, hugging and kissing, enjoying that private and peaceful place.

When they finally left, it was dark. Paul was driving carefully. Everything had been fine. It was late, but the roads were deserted.

Bess didn't want to remember any more, but

now she couldn't stop reliving the accident. The flash of light, the screech of tires. Her own body flying through the air. And then blackness.

The next thing she remembered was George and Nancy leaning over her, crying. Holding her down. George telling her the awful news. Bess couldn't believe it—wouldn't believe it—but she knew it was true. The words repeated themselves in her head: Paul was dead.

Bess wanted to shut out the sight of the blinding white hospital room. But she couldn't stand to shut her eyes. Every time she did, she saw images of Paul's laughing face. The wrinkles at the corner of his eyes. How many times had Bess traced them when they were alone together?

She would never be able to touch them again. To touch him again, or to feel his strong arms around her.

Bess's crying turned to sobs. It seemed impossible that Paul could be dead. Everything about him was still so clear to her.

Bess shook her head. It was starting to pound. All the things she'd wanted to say to him, she would never be able to say now.

"I didn't tell him how special he was," Bess whispered to herself, tears streaming down her cheeks. "I didn't tell him how strong he made me feel. Or how safe."

But why wasn't *he* safe? Bess thought. How could it have been him, and not her? Why?

I didn't tell him often enough how much I cared, Bess realized.

"How much I loved him," she murmured, her heart like a lead weight in her chest, dragging her down.

Bess felt as if she were drowning. She couldn't breathe. Nothing seemed real, not the sheet that covered her, the cast on her arm, the bed she lay in. Not the tubes in her arm, the bandages, the hospital.

She could almost feel him, the warmth of his jacket against her cheek as she held him. But Paul was gone. Forever.

And Bess was alone. What would she do?

Ginny sat in the hospital office waiting for the supervisor of the Wilder volunteer program to arrive. She was nervous about her first day of work, mostly because she wondered whether she would enjoy it.

I hope this gives me some answers, Ginny said to herself. She had been so tired of trying to decide whether she wanted her future to be in medicine or something more creative like music, that when her premed adviser had told her about the volunteer program, Ginny had leaped at the chance to join. Maybe some hands-on experience could help her decide.

If she hated hospital work, well, that would pretty much kill the last flicker of possibility for medical school. And if she loved it?

Let's just wait and see, Ginny told herself.

"Ginny Yuen?" A pleasant-looking woman in a white coat came into the office and held out her hand. "Dr. Ann Gryce," she offered. "I'm pleased to meet you."

Dr. Gryce sat down and pulled out a file. From across the table, Ginny recognized the application she'd filled out for the medical school program.

"Impressive," Dr. Gryce said, raising her eyebrows and skimming Ginny's application appreciatively. "With this kind of record, you should be able to go to any medical school you want."

"Thanks." Ginny smiled.

"Are you thinking of any particular school?" Dr. Gryce asked. "I know quite a bit about the better programs. I'd be happy to talk to you about them."

"I appreciate that," Ginny replied. "But that's partly why I'm here. I'm not sure I still want to go to medical school," she admitted, wondering if it was wise to tell her new boss.

"I can understand that," Dr. Gryce said easily. "It's a big commitment and not one to be made lightly."

"That's how I feel," Ginny told her, happy to see that Dr. Gryce didn't seem put off by her uncertainty. "It's something I've been expected to do for a long time, but now I don't know if I really want to be a doctor."

Dr. Gryce nodded sympathetically. "We'll be

able to offer you an idea of what medicine, and the life of a doctor, will be like," she promised, leaning back in her chair.

"At first you'll spend time in the pediatrics ward," Dr. Gryce explained. "You'll play with the children and help to make them comfortable and keep their spirits up. I know that may not seem like a doctor's job," Dr. Gryce said, noticing Ginny's expression. "But having a caring manner, with real compassion and understanding for your patients is one of the most important qualities you'll need to be a good doctor."

"That makes sense," Ginny said thoughtfully.

"And just so you don't think it's all fun and games"—Dr. Gryce smiled—"you will have an opportunity to observe the doctors and residents at work. You'll even view an operation or two. There's one scheduled for tomorrow, in fact, that I think you'll find quite remarkable. Maybe we can arrange for you to observe it."

"I hope so," Ginny said.

Pam was shocked when she saw the large crowd of women gathered outside the African-American Cultural Alliance Center. The Natural Shades company had set up long tables in front of the building to sign up all the potential candidates.

I never realized I was going to school with so many gorgeous women, Pam thought to herself, her heart sinking as she gazed around the lawn.

Now that she'd seen her competition, Pam almost scolded herself. Why had she ever thought she might win? It was disheartening to see how many attractive women there were just at Wilder. Imagine how many other schools the Natural Shades reps had already visited!

There must be hundreds—no, thousands—of beautiful women out there, Pam realized, dismayed.

She was on the verge of turning around to leave when she heard someone call her name.

Pam scanned the crowd until she saw someone waving frantically in her direction. Pam smiled in surprise and relief when she saw it was Reva Ross, one of Nancy's suitemates.

For some reason Pam was surprised to see Reva in the crowd of hopefuls. Not that she wasn't beautiful. In fact, Pam thought Reva probably had a better chance than she did. Not only did Reva have long, shiny black hair but she had lovely almond-shaped dark eyes, which, against her smooth light brown skin, gave her a captivating look.

"I'm so glad to see you." Reva smiled, taking in the crowd around them. "I was starting to get uneasy standing out here alone. I hope this doesn't take too long, though," Reva admitted. "I had to leave Andy with two of our computer clients this morning. He wasn't exactly thrilled."

"Speaking of which, what made you want to enter this competition?" Pam asked curiously.

"From what I've heard, you're a whiz at school, and you and Andy have a nice little business going as computer consultants."

"I know. But I use Natural Shades products," Reva explained. "And of course, big money is always attractive. Besides," she added, "this sounds like fun. I don't usually get to be anyone other than Reva the computer whiz. I'm so predictable that you just summed up my whole life in one sentence. I wouldn't mind a little glamour and excitement to spice it up."

Why should I be surprised? Pam asked herself. I gave her almost the same speech Jamal gave me.

"If anybody can understand you, it's me," Pam admitted. "I might never have thought of myself as a model, but I'm sure not going to pass up an opportunity to be called gorgeous by the rest of the world!"

Reva laughed and nodded in agreement. "And don't forget the money," she said again, grinning mischievously.

"I couldn't," Pam agreed. "But what would you do about your computer business if you won the Natural Shades search? Would you just drop it?"

"I don't know," Reva admitted. "To be honest, I haven't really thought that far ahead. Looking around, I can't believe I'll even make it past the first cut, so I doubt I'll have to make that choice."

Pam could understand Reva's pessimism. There were a lot of great-looking women all around them. It would be remarkable if Pam got picked out of a crowd this size, let alone the whole Midwest.

But she still couldn't tamp down the flutter of nervous excitement in her stomach as she and Reva approached the tables. Nor did she want to. This was too much fun!

CHAPTER 5

"Nancy, what's taking so long?" Anna asked worriedly, biting her lip and staring at the floor. "What else do they have to ask him?"

Nancy put her arm around Anna's shoulders and gave her a quick hug. A few hours had passed since Anna had called to tell Nancy that her father was in jail. Now Nancy and Anna were at the Weston police station, along with Max Krauser, a Wilder senior who was the head of the Helping Hands program.

"The police just need to make sure that your dad is telling the truth," Nancy explained. "It was a serious accident. Someone was killed. Whoever was driving is going to be in a lot of trouble."

"I'm sure they'll be done soon," Max said,

smiling at Anna encouragingly. "And if there's anything Michael can do to help, he'll do it."

Michael Hill was a lawyer in Weston and a friend of Max's. After Nancy had gotten off the phone with Anna, she'd called Max at Helping Hands to let him know what was happening and to see if he knew someone who could help Mr. Pederson.

Max had phoned Michael before Nancy and Max picked up Anna on their way to the police station. By the time they'd arrived, Michael was already in with Mr. Pederson and the police.

"I wish they'd hurry up," Anna whispered.

Nancy knew Anna was worried, but she was finding it hard to reassure her Little Sister. Nancy had nothing but contempt and anger for the driver who had hit Paul and Bess and driven away without stopping. Nancy realized she shouldn't jump to a conclusion about Mr. Pederson's involvement until she knew all of the facts. But if he was the driver, she was going to be in a very difficult position with Anna.

"They're coming out now," Max said. Michael was walking down the hall toward them with two officers. There was no sign of Mr. Pederson.

"Where's my dad?" Anna asked worriedly.

"He's not free to go yet," Michael said, turning to Nancy and Max. "Let me fill you in on what's happening." Michael pointed to the benches, and they all sat down.

"You know there was a witness who reported the accident?" Michael asked.

Nancy and Max nodded.

"Mr. Pederson's white hatchback fits the witness's description of the car," Michael said. "The partial plate number that the witness reported is also a match," Michael explained. "And it does appear that the car was in an accident recently."

Michael glanced at Anna, and then away. "The front bumper is dented, and there's black paint in the scratches. The police are checking to see if the paint is from the motorcycle that was hit."

"This doesn't sound good," Nancy said.

"But my father couldn't have done it," Anna spoke up.

"Your dad did admit that it might have been his car that hit the motorcycle."

Anna's face went white. Nancy felt numb. She wanted to comfort Anna, but she just couldn't. All Nancy could think about was Bess. And Paul.

"But your father says he's positive he wasn't driving the car," Michael went on gravely. "He claims someone else was in the car with him. Mr. Pederson says he was at a bar—a townie hangout called Blake's Place. And he admits that he had quite a few drinks—"

"Oh, no!" Anna interrupted, sagging against Nancy.

"When he left the bar, a guy in the parking lot asked him for a ride," Michael continued. "Mr. Pederson remembers agreeing to give the guy a ride and taking out his car keys. But then he says the guy offered to drive, and Pederson says he consented. After he got in the car, he claims to have blacked out."

"So Mr. Pederson *might* have been driving," Max said grimly.

"He might have been," Michael admitted. "But when he woke up, he was sitting on the passenger side of his car. And he says his wallet is missing. All of which proves—to him, at least—that someone else was in the car with him."

"But do the police believe him?" Nancy asked.

"I don't know," Michael admitted. "They're still holding him. And since he can't make bail, he'll have to stay in jail."

"What about me?" Anna asked.

"I'm afraid you'll have to be placed in foster care," Michael said. "It's only temporary. A social worker is on her way to the station. She'll take care of you."

"Until they let my father go, right?" Anna asked, looking at Nancy for confirmation. Nancy turned to Michael.

He shrugged. "I hope so," he said sincerely. "Oh, there was one more thing," Michael added. "Pederson said his car smelled of cigarette smoke and there was a matchbook on the dashboard from a Los Angeles bar called the Back Porch."

"But my dad doesn't smoke," Anna said quickly. "Doesn't that prove he's telling the truth?"

"We may have to let a jury decide that."

Nancy hated to see the pain on Anna's face. So much had happened to her in her short life. First she'd lost her mother, and now it looked as if she might lose her father. But Nancy couldn't feel much sympathy for Mr. Pederson. It sure sounded as if he was guilty.

"Anna Pederson?" a woman asked, stepping from the detective's office. "I'm from Child Services. You need to come with me now."

"Nancy, I know my father couldn't have killed anyone," Anna said urgently as she started to leave. "You have to find out who was in the car with him. You have to!"

"I'll do my best," Nancy promised. She watched as Anna was led away down the hall. I feel pretty helpless, she thought. What can I do?

She would check around, but the truth was, she was far from convinced that Mr. Pederson was innocent.

"Thanks for your help," Nancy said, turning back to Max and Michael.

"No problem," Max replied. "We're going to grab some lunch. Why don't you join us."

"Thanks," Nancy replied, "but I'd better get back to campus."

Nancy was on her way out the door when she heard Mr. Pederson's name. She listened to the two police officers who'd interviewed him.

"Yeah, Pederson's in trouble again," one of them said. "It's too bad, isn't it? Ever since his wife died, things have been racing downhill for him."

"Remember those tickets for drunk driving he had back then?" the other officer said.

"And that other accident," the first officer added. "No one was hurt that time, but you can't tempt fate like that."

"Drinking and driving," the second officer said. "If it doesn't kill you, it'll kill someone else."

The other accident? Nancy thought grimly as she hurried out of the police station. Not only did Mr. Pederson have a history of DWI arrests, but he'd already been involved in another car accident?

As bad as she felt for Anna, Nancy couldn't erase the image of Bess lying alone in the hospital, wrapped in bandages. Or the thought of Paul's parents planning a funeral instead of the graduation party they had expected someday.

Nancy shook her head. All in all, the future didn't look very promising for Mr. Pederson. And Nancy hated being in the middle of a situation like this.

"It looks as if those girls aren't making the cut," Pam said. She and Reva watched as several young women with glum expressions were turned away from the tables lined with Natural Shades representatives.

Actually, most of the women who'd come for an interview were dismissed almost immediately.

But a chosen few passed by the tables and entered the AACA Center. Pam and Reva had heard that the Natural Shades reps had set up makeshift studios inside the building where they were doing test photos of a few girls.

"Oh, I've met her," Reva pointed to a tall, slim girl who was making her way into the center. Pam noticed her arrow-straight carriage and long, dark hair.

"She's a knockout," Reva said. "I saw her at the Alpha Delt party last night. Her name is Tamara."

"I guess we should just give up right now," Pam said as Tamara disappeared into the center.

"Oh, come on!" Reva said, grabbing Pam by the arm before she could even pretend to turn around. "I'm not giving up."

Finally Pam found herself face-to-face with a Natural Shades representative. Quickly she filled out a slip of paper with her name and address. Then she glanced up at the rep and waited.

The woman just stared at her.

Isn't she going to ask me any questions? Pam wondered, beginning to feel self-conscious under the woman's sharp scrutiny.

Just as Pam was about to blurt out something, the woman smiled. "Please step inside," she said quickly, already gazing past Pam to the next girl in line.

"Really?" Pam asked, trying to contain her excitement. "Thanks."

Pam took the form and made her way around the table. She looked back just in time to see a happy smile split Reva's face as well.

"Well, at least we weren't dismissed outright," Reva said as she joined Pam at the door to the center.

Inside, Pam was met by a tall, handsome guy wearing a Natural Shades T-shirt. She couldn't help noticing the way it hugged his well-muscled chest.

"Hi," he said, stepping toward her and holding out his hand. "My name is Jesse Potter. I work for Natural Shades."

He led her toward a small side room and motioned to a man with a camera around his neck and five or six more at his feet.

"This is Richard, and believe me, he's an expert photographer of beautiful women." Jesse looked at Pam and smiled. "He'll have no problems with you, so you can just relax."

Pam blushed at the compliment. No matter what Jesse said, though, Pam was nervous. There were about a thousand butterflies in her stomach.

Pam wasn't quite sure what to do when the photographer started snapping pictures. But Jesse, seeing that she was still nervous, started making small talk and asking her questions about herself.

Pam had to admit Jesse's solicitous attention was helpful. He was funny and charming, and of course the fact that he wouldn't stop telling her how lovely she was also helped. Pam finally felt herself begin to relax in front of the camera.

"That's it," Richard finally said, nodding and smiling before he disappeared once more behind his camera.

"Okay." Jesse grinned. "Now you can have fun with it."

Pam couldn't believe it, but she was getting into the mini–photo shoot. Richard was calling out expressions he wanted her to make. Even though the camera was practically in her face, Pam was having fun.

"Good," Richard called out, while Pam changed her mood from silly to serious.

"Are you sure I'm not being too goofy?" Pam asked, raising her eyebrows. But Richard just snapped another shot as Jesse smiled warmly.

"I'm getting a shadow on the right cheek," Richard barked out. "Tilt her head to the left a little."

"This is fun, isn't it?" Jesse whispered, as he stepped closer to Pam. He took her chin in his hand and turned her face away from the lights.

"How's that?" Jesse asked.

"Great," Richard replied as he snapped the shutter.

"It's really fun," Pam said enthusiastically. Then her gaze settled on the door, and she saw Jamal scowling at her from the hall.

"Take your hands off my girlfriend," Jamal barked at Jesse as he came into the room.

Immediately Jesse stepped away from Pam, a surprised expression on his face. Pam opened her mouth to say something, but nothing came out.

"Hey," Jesse said calmly, "nothing's going on here but pictures."

"Well, whatever it is, it's over now," Jamal said, stepping between Jesse and Pam.

"Come on, Pam." Jamal grabbed her hand and started leading her toward the door.

"Whatever you say." Richard shrugged as he put the lens cap back on his camera.

"Jamal?" Pam cried in astonishment and anger. She angrily pulled her hand away. "I can't believe your bad manners," she said and turned toward Jesse and Richard. "You owe Jesse an apology."

"That's okay," Jesse said, trying to ease her embarrassment. "I think we got enough good shots."

"I'm *sure* you got *great* shots," Jamal said tightly. "Come on, Pam. It's time to go."

Pam was so mortified she couldn't even say goodbye as she followed Jamal to the door.

Could this really be happening? Pam wondered. How could Jamal do this to her?

"I'm so glad that's over," Casey said as she and Brian stepped offstage into the wings after their Friday afternoon rehearsal.

"I agree," Brian said. "I don't know who was

out on that stage, but it wasn't me. At least I hope not."

"Maybe no one noticed," Casey said hopefully.

"What were you guys rehearsing for, anyway?" a voice boomed out from above them. "I thought these were one-act plays, not *Night of the Living Dead.*"

Casey looked up. It was Ryan, a lighting technician. He was standing on the catwalk above them, scratching his red beard.

"Oops," Casey muttered, embarrassed. She glanced over at Brian. "Busted."

"Lighting isn't enough for you, huh, Ryan?" Brian joked. "Now you want to be a critic, too?"

Ryan grinned down at them. "Do you want the truth, the whole truth, and nothing but the truth?" he asked.

"Maybe not," Casey replied good-naturedly. She knew Ryan had seen most of the rehearsals. She'd suspected her performance was weak, and if Ryan had noticed, it must have been even worse than she thought.

"We're even getting slammed by the electrician!" Brian moaned theatrically.

"You two are usually the dynamic duo of energy," Ryan said. "And what happened to Bess, the third musketeer? I saw her understudy out there today."

"Didn't you hear about the motorcycle accident?" Casey asked.

"The one outside town?" Ryan asked, surprised. "Sure I did. Was she involved in that?"

Casey nodded.

"That's too bad," Ryan said. "Bess was really good. When you see her, send her my best."

"Thanks," Brian replied. "We're on our way to the hospital now."

Twenty minutes later, after changing, Casey and Brian headed back to Thayer to pick up Casey's car.

"So I guess somebody noticed we were stiff," Casey said. "I know dress rehearsal isn't the best time to give a lame performance, but I just couldn't concentrate."

"Me either," Brian agreed. "I kept thinking about Bess."

"It feels funny to be on stage without her," Casey said. "Especially after all the rehearsing we've done together."

Casey and Brian walked around to the parking lot in back of Thayer Hall.

"Now I know how bummed out I am," Brian said wistfully as they approached Casey's car. "Usually a ride in your MG is the highlight of my week."

"Yeah," Casey agreed. "It doesn't really excite me right now, either. Nothing about driving is very exciting right now."

Brian winced.

"I only wish we had some better news," Casey muttered.

"I can't *believe* Professor Farber won't postpone the performance," Brian complained.

Professor Alan Farber, the director of the one-acts, had heard about the accident and sent Bess his best. But he'd told Casey and Brian before the rehearsal that the show would go on as scheduled—with or without Bess.

"After all the work she put in," Casey said, "it's so unfair she won't be in the production."

"That's not even the worst of it, though," Brian said. "Missing opening night means missing a chance to be chosen for Glasseburg's class. That's *really* going to hurt."

Casey nodded. "I'm sure Glasseburg would have picked Bess after seeing her in the one-acts. Bess could use something to look forward to," Casey said sadly as she and Brian climbed into her car. "Now all we have to give her is bad news."

CHAPTER 6

Where did my parents finally decide to eat dinner?" Bess asked as George walked into her hospital room.

"One of the nurses told them about a decent restaurant nearby," George replied.

"That's good," Bess said, staring out the window at the late afternoon light. "They could probably use a break from here. Hospitals are so depressing."

Bess's parents had arrived from River Heights early that morning. When George got to the hospital that afternoon, she had persuaded Bess's parents to get an early dinner.

"How's it going for you?" George asked, coming to stand over Bess.

"Mom and Dad are trying so hard to cheer me

up," Bess shrugged. "I wish I could feel better, but I don't. How can I?"

"It's going to take time," George admitted. "You know your parents are happy to see that you're okay."

"They're *too* happy," Bess blurted out, feeling guilty even as she spoke. "I mean, I know why. And I'm glad they're here. But all it does is make me think about what Paul's parents must be going through." Bess closed her eyes for a moment. "I feel so helpless."

"I know," George said sympathetically. "Look, is there anything you need? Can I bring you something? Books? Magazines?"

Bess shook her head. She knew her cousin only wanted to help, but everything seemed so unimportant.

"I'm fine," Bess said. "Ginny was here earlier. And Nancy called. She said she was going to stop by before the . . ." Bess stumbled and paused. "The ceremony for Paul tonight," she finished softly.

"Excuse me . . ."

Bess looked up to see a woman standing in the door. Even though Bess had never seen her before, she knew who the woman was. The resemblance between Paul and his mother was unmistakable.

"Are you Bess?" the woman asked, stepping tentatively into the room.

Bess nodded.

"I'm Joan Cody," she explained. "Paul's mother."

"I know," Bess murmured, an image of Paul's face coming to mind. "You have the same eyes." Mrs. Cody smiled slightly, and the laugh lines around her eyes, so much like Paul's, stood out even more.

"Please come in," Bess said.

"I won't stay long," Mrs. Cody went on. "I know you need your rest. But I just wanted to meet the girl Paul talked about so often. He was crazy about you," Mrs. Cody continued, coming to stand over her.

"I loved him," Bess choked out.

"I know," Mrs. Cody said, leaning down. Bess lifted her arms, and they embraced.

"I wish I could come to the funeral," Bess said, sobbing into Mrs. Cody's shoulder, "but I can't leave—"

"Please," Mrs. Cody interrupted her, "don't feel bad. I understand. What matters is what you did for Paul when he was alive."

Mrs. Cody stood up and pulled a tissue from her coat pocket. "I'm sure he told you how he felt," she said, and quickly wiped her eyes. "But I wish you could have heard the way he spoke about you to us. I'd never known him to be so happy."

"I don't know what to do," Bess replied helplessly, staring up at Paul's mother.

"You'll be fine," Mrs. Cody said as she stepped away. "You're a beautiful girl, Bess."

"I don't feel like one right now," Bess answered, lifting a hand to her bruised face.

"But of course you are," Mrs. Cody replied. "Anyone can see that. Paul thought so, too. But, Bess," she added, "he thought much more of you than that. He was always talking about how generous and kind you were, and about everything you did—in your sorority and in the theater department."

Bess felt tears roll down her cheeks.

"I know how hopeless you must feel," Mrs. Cody continued, tears filling her eyes. "But, please," she begged, putting her hand on Bess's good arm. "Don't give up on the life you still have. I know, from what Paul said, that it's rich and full. Your family and friends will help you through this," she added, glancing at George.

Mrs. Cody glanced at Bess one last time, then turned and hurried out the door.

"No wonder he was so special," Bess said, feeling sadder than ever.

Regardless of what Paul's mother said, Bess didn't know how she'd get over this horrible grief and emptiness. She was alive and Paul was dead, and Bess couldn't imagine life without him.

"He said he was coming out, right?" Nancy asked, as she and Jake stood on the sidewalk in front of Blake's Place.

"He had a couple of customers," Jake replied, stroking Nancy's arm. "He'll be out in a minute. Don't worry."

"I'm sorry," Nancy said, resting her head on Jake's shoulder. "I'm anxious."

"This isn't just another story," Jake said sympathetically. "This is personal. It's okay to be anxious."

Nancy had already called Blake's Place and found out that the bartender was the same one who'd been working the night of the accident. She and Jake had decided to ask him a few questions on their way to the hospital.

Besides being a popular bar with the Weston townspeople, Blake's Place was also a hangout for Wilder employees and graduate students.

"Are you looking for me?" The door to Blake's Place opened, and a man in his fifties came out.

"You're Pete?" Nancy smiled. "We spoke on the phone earlier. My name is Nancy, and I'm a reporter with the *Wilder Times*. May I ask you a few questions about last night?"

Pete looked around and sighed. "What can I tell you that I haven't already told the police? I don't know anything about that motorcycle accident."

"I'm sure you told them everything," Nancy agreed. "But if you wouldn't mind telling me again for the newspaper, I'd really appreciate it.

We're doing a story on the accident, since it involved Wilder students," Nancy said.

"Now, we know the suspected driver was in your bar the night of the accident. Do you remember anything about him?" Nancy began. "His name is Pederson. Medium build, thin blond hair? I think he was drinking quite a lot."

"Yeah, sure, I remember him," Pete said, nodding. "Like I told the cops, he got pretty wasted."

"He did?" Nancy asked.

"Yep. He was screaming and carrying on about how he lost his job. He got too rowdy, and I cut him off," Pete said. "I told him to go home and get some sleep. I'm not responsible for what happened after that," he added.

"Would you say he was definitely too drunk to drive?" Nancy asked.

"Look, I did what I could," Pete said warily. "I stopped serving him. I offered to call him a cab. But I can't leave work every time some drunk needs a ride home."

"We understand," Jake said quickly. "We're not here to get you in trouble."

"Just a few more questions," Nancy pressed, seeing that Pete was anxious to get back to work. "Was Mr. Pederson talking to anybody in particular? Any friend of his in the bar? Someone he knew?"

"That guy was talking to anybody and everybody," Pete said exasperated. "I've got to get back inside," he added.

"When Pederson left the bar," Nancy asked quickly, "did anyone leave with him?"

"Nope," Pete answered, stepping toward the door. Then he paused and frowned thoughtfully. "Wait a minute. There was someone. . . . That's right, somebody was leaving then. Not *with* him but at the same time. He's kind of a regular. Tall guy, red hair and a beard. His first name is Ryan," Pete added. "I don't know his last name, but he's young, so I guess he could have been a student."

"And did you notice if he smoked?" Nancy asked, her heart beating faster.

"Honey," Pete said, "in my bar, it smells like everyone smokes. Now I really gotta get back."

"Okay." Nancy smiled warmly. "We appreciate your help."

Nancy watched Pete disappear back into the bar. She stared at the door for a minute.

"I don't know," Nancy said thoughtfully, turning to Jake. "If Mr. Pederson was the one who hit Bess and Paul, I have no sympathy for him."

"It sounds as if he was too drunk to drive," Jake agreed.

"But if he's innocent . . ." Nancy let the sentence hang. "Mr. Pederson may have been telling the truth—at least about someone leaving the bar with him."

"And maybe someone did ask him for a ride," Jake added.

"But that still doesn't prove that he wasn't the

driver," Nancy finished. "There's only one way to find out. The next step is to find this Ryan."

George looked at the expression on her cousin's face and sighed. She almost knew what Bess was thinking.

Mrs. Cody was amazing, George thought, her heart going out to the older woman. After losing her son, she had been kind enough to visit Bess and offer words of love and advice.

"Knock, knock," Brian said, poking his head in through the doorway.

Casey stuck her head in right above his. "Are you up to more visitors?" she asked.

Bess smiled weakly and nodded.

"Hi, George," Brian said, looking both sympathetic and worried.

"How are you feeling? Any better?" Casey asked.

"A little," Bess said. Brian came over to her side and took one of her hands in his.

"We just finished dress rehearsal," Casey said.

"We were terrible," Brian said. "Even the lighting technician noticed the difference."

"And everyone misses you," Casey said. "It wasn't the same, having to work with your understudy."

"My understudy," Bess repeated, staring down at her blankets.

It was almost a question, but there wasn't much emotion behind it. To George it seemed that Bess was barely keeping up with the conversation.

"We were hoping that Alan would decide to postpone the plays," Brian explained. "But he can't."

"The show must go on and all that," Casey said softly, trying to grin but failing.

"Sure," Bess replied indifferently, her expression barely changing.

I can't believe this is Bess, George thought, staring down at her. It seemed impossible that her once vibrant cousin could be so listless and unemotional. Bess had been so passionate and excited about the one-act plays, and especially about opening night. Now it seemed as if she didn't care about missing it.

"Wait a minute," George said suddenly. "How is that acting coach going to see her?"

Casey and Brian turned from George to Bess and then back again. Then they slowly shook their heads.

"She won't," Brian admitted.

Quickly George turned to Bess, but her expression was the same. George thought she hadn't even registered the comment. But then Bess shrugged.

"Whatever," Bess muttered. "It hardly matters anyway."

Brian stepped over to Bess and put his hand on her arm.

George was worried. This wasn't just a grieving

Bess or an upset Bess. This was a Bess Marvin George had never seen in eighteen years together. This Bess was empty of almost every feeling but one.

George hoped that, with time, Bess's happy, spirited personality would return. But that didn't seem possible when she was so full of despair.

"Look, I told you I was sorry," Jamal said, pacing the room, exasperated.

Pam glared at him from her bed. They were in her dorm room, and Pam was still fuming about the scene Jamal had made with the Natural Shades representatives.

"I know I was wrong to storm in that way," Jamal said. "But I didn't like the way that guy was coming on to you, Pam. Can you blame me?"

Pam sighed. "Jamal," she said wearily, "he wasn't coming on to me. He was doing his job. I was nervous, and he was trying to help me relax for the camera."

"But, Pam, he had his hands all over you!" Jamal cried.

"Because the photographer asked him to move my head," Pam explained for the tenth time. "Come on, Jamal, do you think they're in it together? That they made a secret flirting pact?" Pam almost laughing at the idea. "Don't be silly. They see hundreds of girls more beautiful than me every day. You probably ruined any chance I had of getting called back."

"I'm sorry," Jamal said softly. "But it's for the best. You don't really want to be a model."

"Jamal!" Pam cried, exasperated. "Stop it. Don't tell me what I want to do. Just apologize and shut up, all right?"

"Okay," Jamal said again. He came over to her and took her hand. "Anyway, no one is more beautiful than you."

"Now *that's* the correct way to make up," Pam said sternly. But she couldn't prevent a smile from slipping onto her face. Before she could say any more, the phone rang.

"Hello," she murmured as she leaned over and grabbed the receiver.

"Is this Pam Miller?" the voice asked.

"Jesse?" Pam replied, her heart starting to beat excitedly. "Is that you?"

"It's me," Jesse Potter replied. "I'm calling to let you know that we've taken a look at the test pictures."

"And?" Pam held her breath.

"And"—Jesse chuckled—"we'd like you to come back for more photos. This time we'll have you made up with some of our Natural Shades products. Can you make it tomorrow?"

"Of course," Pam replied excitedly as the door to her room opened and George came in. Pam noticed how worn out George looked and sent her a quick smile.

"Hold on a sec. Let me check the schedule and I'll tell you exactly when to be here," Jesse said.

"How's Bess?" Jamal asked as George shrugged out of her coat and tossed it on her bed.

"She's going to be fine, physically," George replied sadly. "The damage is mostly mental. Right now her spirits are really low."

"We'll visit her early tomorrow afternoon," Jamal replied, turning to Pam.

"I don't know if I can go in the early afternoon," Pam said, her hand over the mouthpiece. "I have a callback for the Natural Shades contest. But I'll visit Bess right after I'm through."

George paused and gave her an annoyed look. "Whatever," she replied. "Don't strain yourself," she added as she turned back to her closet.

"Look, George, I'm sorry," Pam began, knowing her roommate was upset. "What happened is terrible, but—"

"Pam?" Jesse's voice interrupted.

"Just a sec," Pam whispered to George and Jamal. "Yes?"

"I've got you on the list," Jesse began. "It'll probably take a few hours. Why don't you come at noon?"

"Great!" Pam replied excitedly. "And, Jesse, thanks a lot for helping me this afternoon."

She heard George clear her throat angrily, and Pam winced. She could understand why George was mad at her. It probably seemed heartless that Pam was happy about anything when Bess was in the hospital and Paul was dead. But Pam was also truly sorry about what had happened to her

79

friends, and she knew that altering her own plans wasn't going to change the sad outcome of the accident.

First Jamal and now George, Pam thought, shaking her head. Is my being in this modeling contest so bad? Why should I give up the most exciting opportunity I've ever had?

CHAPTER 7

"Y ou ready?" Jake asked Nancy as he helped her on with her coat.

"No," Nancy replied, pushing her arms through the sleeves. "But I don't think I ever would be." Nancy took a candle in one hand and Jake's hand in the other. Their fingers twined. Jake leaned over and gave her a kiss.

"It's time to go," he said softly.

In the hall outside Suite 301, the students were gathering in a somber group. Without saying anything, they all silently agreed to go to the candlelight vigil together. Everyone needed to be with friends.

"I can't believe this is happening," Reva said, taking Andy's arm. "It's like a bad dream."

Nancy felt raw inside. Bess was one of her

closest friends. "Reva's right, it *is* a nightmare," she murmured.

Jake just shook his head, unable to express his sadness.

The walk to the quad was very quiet. Many students were coming from their dorms and heading for the vigil. But the chatty clamor that usually followed people to classes had been replaced with silence.

It was a cool, moonless night. Nancy's throat was tight, and her vision was blurred with tears. She took Jake's arm and gave it a squeeze. Kara walked arm in arm with her boyfriend, Tim Downing. Reva was with Andy Rodriguez, as Ginny and Ray walked beside them. Liz and Daniel were nearby with Eileen, Stephanie, Casey, Brian, and Brian's friend Chris Vogel. Dawn and Bill were close behind.

Besides her friends, Nancy saw classmates whose names she didn't know, and a few of her professors. Bess's sorority sisters were walking together, with Kappa vice president Holly Thornton leading the group.

And of course Paul's fraternity brothers, the Zetas, were out in force. Emmet trailed behind the others. Eileen split off from the pack and walked over to take his hand.

Nearing the lake, Nancy felt someone take her other arm. It was George. Will was walking beside her, staring straight ahead. Nancy could see that George had been crying, but Will's face was a mask, revealing nothing. Everyone knew by now that it was his motorcycle Paul had died on.

"Will," Nancy began, then stopped herself. Don't do this to yourself, she said to him with her eyes.

Will turned away, his expression still steely, his hands balled into fists.

Down at the lake, Nancy saw large groups of people standing around in a loose circle. The candles were spread across the expanse like the lights of a distant city.

Squeezing her eyes shut, Nancy conjured up a picture of Paul in her mind: his golden hair and his soft, sensitive brown eyes. His eyes were flanked by deep laugh lines. He was always laughing.

That's how Nancy wanted to remember him: laughing.

She looked down into the sea of candles and, squeezing Jake's hand, whispered quietly, "Goodbye, Paul."

If only Bess could be here, George thought as she gazed at the soft yellow lights flickering against the black water in front of them.

But that wasn't really true, George realized. The truth was that while she was moved to see the outpouring of concern from so many people, she wished none of them were here.

"I feel so helpless," George said, leaning into

the circle of Will's arms. She turned to Nancy beside her.

"Do you really think that Anna's father caused the accident?" George asked.

Nancy shrugged. "I don't know," she admitted. "Mr Pederson was definitely too drunk to be driving."

"But the bartender did say that some guy left the bar at the same time," Jake added. "Which could mean that Pederson's story about someone else driving the car might be true."

"The other guy was a regular," Nancy explained. "And the bartender said he was young, so he could be from the university."

"You mean a student might have been driving the car?" George asked.

"If Mr. Pederson is telling the truth," Nancy replied. "But he's not the most reliable witness, since he doesn't remember anything."

"I hope they lock the guy up and throw away the key!" Will burst out vehemently.

"I do, too," Nancy said, laying a hand on Will's arm. "I get mad every time I think about it, too."

"We're going to find this guy the bartender told us about," Jake added. "Maybe he was involved. Or maybe the police already have the person responsible."

"As bad as I feel for Anna, if her father caused that accident," Nancy said, "I can't forgive him. And if what I heard about his record is true, he'll have a long time to think about what he did."

"Maybe," Will said, obviously upset.

"What do you mean?" George asked.

"Who am I kidding," Will suddenly moaned, breaking free of George's arm. "They never should have been out on the road in the first place. The whole thing is my fault!"

"Your fault?" George asked. "Will, stop it, what are you saying?"

"Why?" he asked sharply, slapping his thigh with his fist. "Why did I let them take my motorcycle?"

"Will!" George cried, reaching for him. He pushed away from her, threw his candle onto the damp grass, and stalked off into the crowd.

George was about to run after him when she felt a hand gripping her arm.

"Let him go," Jake said softly, putting his other hand on George's shoulder.

"Did you hear him?" George asked. "How can he think he's responsible? That's crazy."

"Everyone's upset about the accident," Nancy replied. "Maybe Will's way of dealing with it right now is to be angry. I know he feels terrible about Bess and Paul," Nancy said thoughtfully. "But maybe that's not all that's upsetting him."

George looked at her in confusion. "What are you talking about?"

"How many times have you been on the back of Will's motorcycle with him?" Nancy asked.

"A lot," George answered without thinking. She watched Will as he moved toward the lake.

"Exactly," Nancy said.

"So what does that mean?" George asked, trying to keep her eyes on Will's back as he made his way down to the edge of the water.

"Sometimes it's easier to get angry than to think about what you've lost," Nancy replied. "Or what you are afraid of losing."

"You think he's worried about me?" George asked. "But I'm fine."

"The accident was a fluke," Nancy said. "And perhaps there's no reason, except bad luck, that it was Bess and Paul out there and not you and Will," she added. "Maybe that's what Will's really feeling guilty about. He doesn't want to think about how many times you've been on that bike with him. Or how afraid he would be to lose you."

George hadn't thought of it, but now that Nancy pointed it out, it made a weird kind of sense. Statistically speaking, it *could* have been Will and her in the accident. No wonder Will was so torn up. George looked out at all the flickering candles reflected in the water and shuddered.

As Ginny and Ray walked back from the lake after the vigil for Paul, Ginny couldn't help noticing how upset Ray was. She squeezed his fingers in understanding. They were all shocked by the accident, and Ginny was really glad that Ray had taken the time to come with her to the vigil. But she had a feeling Ray was thinking about more than Paul.

"What's wrong?" she asked gently. "It isn't just about the accident, is it?"

"I'm worried about our album deal," Ray admitted guiltily. "We just sent Pacific Records a tape of two new songs we want to do on the album. They called and said they wanted to discuss the new songs—in person. I sent Spider to L.A. to meet with one of their execs."

Spider was a member of the Beat Poets and one of Ray's best friends, and Spider's brother was the band's manager.

"So what are you worried about?" Ginny asked, confused. "Don't you trust Spider?"

"Sure," Ray said. "I couldn't go to L.A. myself because I have to finish this huge paper by Monday," he moaned. "If I don't get at least a C, I could fail the class."

"Well," Ginny said, "it's just a matter of priorities. You can't beat yourself up about this paper. You—"

"Look," Ray interrupted. "I'm not trying to slack off. But I promised myself that school wasn't going to get in the way of my music."

"I know," Ginny said, somehow feeling guilty because she was the one who didn't want him to drop out of school. But she was also hurt by his tone of voice. "You already said you might drop out," she added, hurt and angry. "You don't have to get mad at me. Just do it and stop complaining."

"I'm not mad at you," Ray said carefully. "And I still may drop out," he added. "I haven't decided. But if I leave Wilder, I want it to be my choice. I don't want to flunk out," he said. "I'm not an idiot."

"Well, neither is Spider," Ginny replied. "Everything will be fine."

"But it's my band," Ray mumbled. "I'm the one who should be in L.A. Besides," he complained, "I'm having a hard time with this stupid paper. Who knows if I'll even get it done? I probably should have just scrapped it and gone to L.A. myself."

"I have doubts about what to do, too," Ginny said, trying to help. "But dropping out of school isn't necessarily the answer. I just started that volunteer program—"

"Why? Why keep following your original plan when you don't want to go to med school?" Ray asked, frustrated.

"It's not a rigid plan, Ray," Ginny said defensively. "I'm trying to figure out what *I* want."

"You have doubts, but you won't give up being premed. It's just like me and music," he argued. "I'm willing to go for the dream, and you're sitting here telling me to make sure I finish school."

"It's not like that!" Ginny cried. "You should be prepared—"

"I'm prepared to make music my life's work,"

Ray said. "And I need all my energy for that. You're just too scared, Ginny. You should be doing something creative, too."

"But that's what I'm trying to tell you," she argued back. "You just won't listen. Medicine *is* creative. When I was at the hospital with those kids, it felt so rewarding—"

"Doing that is safe," Ray interrupted. "Ginny, come on! Don't fool yourself, it's just baby-sitting."

"How can you say that!" Ginny asked, shocked at how mean Ray sounded. "You don't even know what I do, because you don't listen anymore. You just don't care."

"I care," Ray replied. "I care about you. But I'm not going to get stuck here!" he added, yelling at her as though she were the one holding him back.

"I don't care where you get stuck!" Ginny yelled back, her anger and disappointment wrestling for control.

They'd both stopped and were standing opposite each other like boxers.

"You're not the same," Ray said. "This isn't you."

"It *is* me," Ginny snapped. "Maybe you just can't accept that."

"This is the conservative you," Ray said coolly. "And you're just going to let that part win. You're going to do what your parents want and try to convince yourself that you're happy."

89

Ginny was shocked at how quickly things had gotten so bad between them. She almost couldn't believe this was the same guy she loved.

"I don't *have* to convince myself that I'm *unhappy*," Ginny replied, her voice like ice. "Right at this moment. With you."

"Well, you shouldn't have to do anything you don't want to," Ray said sarcastically. "So don't let me ruin your evening."

With that he turned away and stalked off into the darkness. Surprisingly, Ginny wasn't sad to see him go.

Bill and Dawn made their way back to Thayer along with Casey, Stephanie, Nancy, and Jake. "I'm really glad Zach's here this weekend," Bill said. "It's been great to see him again."

"I bet." Dawn smiled. "You two have been acting like a couple of . . . high schoolers, actually."

"He takes me back. And after tonight, I realize how important it is to make every minute count," Bill said, giving her hand a quick squeeze.

"I agree," Dawn said. The ceremony that night had been really moving for her.

Dawn was more sure of her decision than before, and she was committed to making her relationship with Bill something special. She could hardly wait to tell him.

When they reached the dorm, Dawn saw Zach standing outside, smoking a cigarette. He nodded when he spotted them, and as they came closer and Zach saw who they were with, his face lit up.

"Zach does have an eye for the ladies," Bill said.

"Just keep him away from my freshmen," Dawn warned.

"I'll take care of this one," Jake replied, draping an arm over Nancy's shoulder. "But those two are your trouble," he added, nodding to Casey and Stephanie, who had already detached themselves from the group and were walking over to Zach.

"Hello, Casey," Zach said, sounding pleasantly surprised. "Stephanie."

Dawn had to smile as she watched the way Zach operated with two beautiful women hanging on his every word. He managed to give each of them the same number of penetrating gazes, and he flashed his quirky smile in each girl's direction exactly the same number of times. He was smooth.

"He's quite the ladies' man, isn't he?" Nancy said, noticing Dawn's watchful gaze.

"He looks like a movie star," Dawn agreed.

"Exactly," Bill replied, overhearing the two women. "That's even his nickname. Everyone in high school used to call him the Star."

"And he probably wasn't embarrassed about it at all," Dawn guessed.

"Nope," Bill agreed. "He loved his reputation. He even wore sunglasses twenty-four hours a day. Winter, summer, in the classroom, on the basketball court."

"Well, he must have changed a little," Nancy commented. "He's grown out of that phase. I can see his gorgeous blue eyes from here."

"Hey!" Jake cried, pulling Nancy against his chest.

"You have nothing to worry about," Dawn heard Nancy say.

"Zach hasn't changed," Bill explained. "I noticed it right away, and he told me he just lost a pair of sunglasses."

"Left them buried on some exotic beach, I guess," Dawn remarked. "Ah, for the life of a world traveler."

"I don't know," Nancy said. "Traveling is pretty lonely most of the time."

"Unless you're Zach," Bill pointed out.

"Well, I'm glad you're not Zach," Dawn said quickly. "I like you the way you are."

"Thanks." Bill smiled at her.

"This was a difficult night," Nancy said, leaning close to Jake. "But I'd still rather be here than anywhere else."

"I have to agree," Dawn said. She turned back to Bill and gave his fingers a squeeze.

And pretty soon you'll know why, she thought.

CHAPTER 8

When Reva woke up the next morning, she was still melancholy. The vigil for Paul had been very sad.

Reva turned her head and saw that Eileen was awake and staring up at the ceiling.

"Hey there," Reva croaked out. She cleared her throat to get rid of her morning voice.

Eileen looked over and a smile lit her freckled face. "It's nice to see you, roomie," she said meaningfully.

"Last night was really intense, wasn't it?" Reva said, recalling the haze of candlelight around the lake. "I don't think I've ever seen anything so beautiful."

"Yes, it was really nice," Eileen replied. "The vigil was Emmet's idea."

"I was amazed at how many people showed up," Reva said. "Paul couldn't have known them all personally."

"No," Eileen said. "I think a lot of people came just to show they cared. I heard lots of people on campus talking about the accident. I think everyone was pretty touched. It's a tragedy for the whole university that someone like Paul is gone."

"He was such a sweet guy," Reva agreed.

"Anyway," Eileen said, "after last night, and all the love people were sharing, it almost doesn't seem fair to be gloomy. Besides, I haven't really seen you in days. You have to get that boyfriend of yours to hang out here more often," Eileen complained.

"But he's got all the computer stuff in his and Will's apartment," Reva said.

"And his own bedroom," Eileen added. "Don't try to defend yourself to me. I know you have more privacy there. So what's going on?"

"It's kind of weird to feel happy about something now," Reva admitted. "But remember that Natural Shades contest I mentioned?"

"The one that's going to put you on the cover of *Vogue* and *Glamour?*" Eileen smiled.

"They called me back for a second interview," Reva said.

"Really!" Eileen grinned, tossing a pillow across the room at her. "I wonder why," she teased.

94

"Hey!" Reva threw the pillow back.

"I'm kidding," Eileen said. "It's great news. Aren't you psyched?"

"Well, I've always been the 'brain' of the family. So it is pretty nice to think of myself as glamorous, too."

"Just don't get cocky on me, roomie," Eileen warned good-naturedly. "What are you going to wear?"

"I don't know," Reva said. "What do you think?"

"Stand back and let the Wilder fashion queen guide you," Eileen joked, pulling herself out of bed and heading for Reva's closet.

"So, the candlelight vigil was Emmet's idea?" Reva asked, recalling what Eileen had said. "It was amazing. How's he holding up?"

Eileen stopped digging through Reva's clothes and sighed.

"He's taking it pretty hard," she said. "Paul was his closest friend. And he's been helping the Codys pack Paul's things. I know that has to be rough," Eileen said softly.

"It must be hard on all of them," Reva agreed.

"But good for them, too," Eileen went on hopefully. "They're sort of helping each other through it. Bess is the one I'm really worried about," Eileen admitted. "I can't imagine what she must be going through."

Reva thought of her own boyfriend and shivered. She didn't want to imagine what life would be like without Andy.

A lot more lonely for one thing, she told herself.

"I'm almost embarrassed to admit this," Eileen continued, draping several of Reva's dresses over her arm. "But in a weird way, this whole thing has brought Emmet and me much closer." Eileen shrugged and tossed a velvet shirt at Reva.

"I bet it's really important to him to have your support right now," Reva said.

"I think so," Eileen said. "But I don't mean just right now. This tragedy has put our whole relationship in perspective. Everything we've disagreed about—our argument about modern art, for instance—seems so trivial now," Eileen continued. "I mean, when you think about life and death, who really cares what a slash of red paint on a black canvas is supposed to mean?"

"But you shouldn't belittle the things that make you happy," Reva said.

"No," Eileen agreed. "I don't mean that. Of course I'll always love modern art. And Emmet will probably always hate it. I just mean that what matters is that two people care about each other," Eileen explained. "Not the annoying little things that sometimes get in the way."

"I think I know what you're saying," Reva replied.

Reva thought of the Natural Shades contest. She wasn't embarrassed to admit it was exciting.

And Reva couldn't deny that she'd already daydreamed about winning. But even if she didn't win, she'd still have school. And the computer business. And Andy.

Reva sighed as she thought of her boyfriend. Andy was amazing—smart, funny, gorgeous, driven. Exactly the kind of guy she'd always wanted. She was so lucky to have found him.

No question that modeling and making tons of money was fun to dream about. But doing well in school and spending time with Andy—that was what made her life worth living.

"I can't say I'm looking forward to tonight's performance," Nancy admitted. She broke off the end of her croissant and popped it in her mouth. Nancy and George were at Java Joe's for breakfast, but there was a pall hanging over them. Usually there were three of them at their Saturday morning breakfast meetings. It didn't feel complete without Bess.

"I know what you mean," George replied, taking a quick sip of coffee. "I'm sure it'll be fun, and we promised Bess we'd go, but it's going to be strange watching someone else play her part."

"At least we can show our support for Casey and Brian," Nancy said.

"Speaking of whom, there's Brian now." George glanced over at the door. "He doesn't look very psyched about tonight, either."

Nancy had to agree. Brian looked as sad and

97

exhausted as she felt. She was starting to wave him over when she noticed he had stopped to talk to a guy at a nearby table. They exchanged a few words, and then Brian nodded and walked on.

Nancy was about to turn away when something clicked in her mind. The guy Brian had been talking to had red hair and a beard. That was how the bartender had described the person who left Blake's Place with Mr. Pederson the night of the accident!

Not that Nancy should assume the first person she saw who fit the description was the one she was looking for, but then again, red hair and a beard weren't exactly common. Nancy told George she'd be right back and walked over to the counter.

"Brian, who was that guy you were just talking to?" Nancy asked.

"Who, Ryan?" Brian said. "He's one of the lighting technicians for the one-act plays."

Nancy couldn't believe her luck. Ryan was also the name of the guy Pete had told her about.

"Do you know him?" Brian asked. Nancy was about to explain it to him, but then she noticed his distracted expression and Nancy could see his mind was elsewhere.

"Thinking about tonight?" Nancy guessed.

"Yeah," Brian said. "It's going to be weird. And now I can't seem to remember any of my lines."

"You're going to be great tonight," Nancy assured him. "We'll all be there."

"Everyone except Bess," Brian muttered. "But thanks for the support."

Nancy watched Brian walk away. She knew how much he cared for Bess, and she just hoped he'd be able to pull himself together for the performance.

On her way back to George, Nancy picked out a path that would take her by Ryan's table. She wanted to get a closer look at him.

Nancy slowed as she passed. She looked down and saw a pack of cigarettes on the table. And a matchbook. Nancy glanced at it quickly and almost stumbled. It was a black matchbook with neon orange lettering: The Back Porch.

The matchbook was the same as the matches the police had found in Mr. Pederson's car after the accident!

While she was staring down at his table, Ryan looked up.

"Hello?" he asked. "Can I help you?" He followed her gaze and then smiled. "Need a light?"

"Oh, no," Nancy said quickly, shaking her head. This was a great opportunity to speak to him, Nancy realized. Don't blow it, she told herself, putting a bright smile on her face.

"I'm sorry," Ryan said. "Do I know you?"

"You do now." Nancy smiled. "I'm Nancy Drew. You look familiar," Nancy continued, pausing and then snapping her fingers. "Haven't I seen you at Blake's Place?" she asked innocently.

Immediately Ryan's expression became guarded.

"Maybe," he said slowly. "I've been there. But I don't remember you."

"But just a few nights ago," Nancy pressed. "On Thursday. Weren't you there Thursday night? You'd remember," Nancy added, watching him closely. "The night of that awful accident?"

For a moment Ryan appeared to be startled. Then he shrugged and stood up.

"Listen, I'd love to talk," he said, pulling on his coat. "But I've got to get back to work. We have an opening tonight. Sorry."

Ryan reached down to grab his cigarettes and the matchbook. He slipped them in his pocket.

Nancy watched him push his way through the crowd and slip out the door. Her mind was racing. His manner had certainly changed when she asked questions about Thursday night. He'd been too suspicious and much too anxious to get away from what should have been pretty harmless questions.

At least she knew who he was, Nancy realized, heading back to George. And she knew where to find him.

"So, did you learn anything useful?" George asked, as soon as Nancy got back to their table. Nancy related her conversation with Ryan.

"He was pretty nervous when it came to talking about Blake's Place," Nancy said thoughtfully.

"And there wouldn't be any reason for him to act so nervous," George began.

"Unless he had something to hide," Nancy finished grimly.

You once pledged, on your life, not to spend one minute more than you had to in Dullstown, U.S.A., Stephanie reminded herself about Berrigan's. So why are you so eager to get to work?

It wasn't even nine o'clock on Saturday morning and she was already toweling off in the steamy bathroom. The suite was quiet; everyone else was either still asleep or at breakfast.

Stephanie looked at herself in the fogged mirror and noticed something she hadn't seen in a long time: real excitement.

And she couldn't pretend not to know exactly why her eyes were bright and her skin a little more flushed than usual. Dinner with Jonathan before the memorial service for Paul had been really great, Stephanie admitted to herself.

After wrapping herself in a purple bath sheet, Stephanie pushed through the bathroom door, humming. For the first time her job didn't feel like a drag on her social life—or her life in general, for that matter. Maybe Jonathan was her social life? Knowing she would see him actually made Stephanie eager to get to work.

He might ask me to dinner again, she thought eagerly, then suddenly stopped.

Zach was standing in the hallway by the

lounge, staring at her. Quickly Stephanie cinched the bath sheet tighter around her slim body. "What are *you* doing here?"

"I was looking for you," he replied easily.

"How did you get in here?" Stephanie asked.

Zach ran his fingers through his sun-streaked hair. "Someone was going to breakfast. Kara? She said you were in the shower, so . . ."

"So," Stephanie began, unable to stop the flutter in her stomach. Zach was really hot. "I'm on my way to work," Stephanie finished.

Zach's blue eyes darkened with disappointment. "That's too bad. Because Bill is busy with some R.A. thing, which leaves me with a free day. . . ." He smiled. "I was hoping to spend it with you. I heard there was a place to go bungee-jumping around here."

"Me? Bungee-jump?" Stephanie snorted. "Sorry."

"Come on, it's a trip!" Zach insisted. "Once you get over your initial fear, you think you're flying. The only thing that's better is skydiving. And there's nobody I'd rather hurtle through the air with," he teased, the corner of his mouth curling into a sexy grin.

Stephanie couldn't ignore the little leap of feeling in the pit of her stomach—not at the thought of jumping off a bridge and hurtling toward the water or ground or something flat and hard and painful, but at the look Zach was giving her—one hundred percent pure appreciation.

"I have to work," she repeated.

"You couldn't blow it off?" Zach asked, gazing at her intently.

Well, it helps that you're standing here naked under a towel, Stephanie reminded herself, embarrassed at how easily she'd just imagined skipping work. Wasn't it only a minute ago that she was actually eager to get to Berrigan's? How could two guys make her feel so similar?

But did she really feel the same way about them? Stephanie wondered. She thought of Jonathan and smiled. It wasn't the same feeling; with Jonathan the little leaps were in her heart.

Stephanie shook her head. "Sorry," she said. "I'm hanging by a, um, bungee cord already."

Zach shrugged, his expression pouty with disappointment. "Maybe next time."

"Maybe next time what?" a voice asked.

Stephanie turned to find Casey leaning her tall frame in the doorway to their room, rubbing her eyes. Holding her toothbrush in one hand, she was barefoot in a robe and her sleeping T-shirt, and she still had that infuriatingly enticing wind-blown look. Stephanie observed that Zach didn't fail to notice, either.

"Bungee-jumping," he said. "Fresh air, excitement, a great picnic. What do you say?"

"Me?" Casey said, alarmed.

Stephanie laughed. "That's what I said."

"It's totally safe," Zach insisted. "I guarantee it."

Something else Stephanie couldn't fail to notice was the way Casey was checking out Zach.

"Hmm," Casey said, "let me think about it." She pointed her toothbrush toward the bathroom door and followed it. Stephanie followed her.

"You actually want to go?" she asked, standing next to Casey at the mirror.

"Why not?" Casey replied with a mouthful of toothpaste. "I only have a lit paper to write for next week. And an opening-night performance in ten hours. Nothing I haven't blown off before," Casey joked.

Stephanie eyed her roommate in the mirror. "It's kind of interesting that you're so willing to go out on a date with another guy, considering you're engaged."

Casey raised an eyebrow. "Date? Who said date? It's just a day of fresh air, excitement—"

"Yeah, yeah, and a great picnic," Stephanie finished with a conspiratorial chuckle.

"What's the harm in an afternoon with a friend?" Casey asked, then murmured: "It's not my fault he happens to be an amazingly *hunky* friend."

"Exactly." Stephanie nodded.

Casey leaned down and rinsed her mouth. "Look," she said, "this thing with Bess has gotten me depressed. It's shown me how short life can be. We need to really live, because you never know . . ."

"Nice thought." Stephanie smirked.

"I've been trying to reach Charley on location for the last two days," Casey said a little defensively. "But I can't get through. Besides, do I need his permission to go to a theme park? What's wrong with a little company to cheer me up? It's totally innocent, Steph."

Casey stepped across the hall to their room, with Stephanie right behind her. "You're on," Casey called out to Zach. "Just let me get changed."

"You look good to me," Zach commented from the hallway.

"Did you hear that?" Stephanie said, locking the door behind her.

"Hear what?" Casey said. She hurriedly stepped into a fresh pair of jeans and pulled on a bulky sweater.

"Just for the record, roomie, I think this is a mistake," Stephanie said soberly.

Casey shook out her hair, not registering the comment. "See you later," she said breezily. She grabbed a jacket and left.

Stephanie sat on the edge of her bed, amazed at her sudden realization: Casey was spending the day with a guy who not only asked her out first, but was gorgeous, intriguing, smart, and daring. All the qualities Stephanie usually enjoyed in a man, not to mention a date.

And I don't feel a bit jealous, she thought, a slow smile playing across her lips.

Obviously Stephanie felt more for Jonathan than she'd thought, and that realization surprised her. The only thing she had to do now was ignore the small shiver of worry that came with it.

CHAPTER 9

"Yum," Bess said unenthusiastically as she lifted a forkful of soggy rice to her mouth. Before it got halfway, she let it drop back to the tray. Hospital food was living up to its reputation as bland and inedible. She didn't have the energy or the spirit to eat, anyway.

Early afternoon sunlight streamed through the curtains, playing on her blankets and warming her face. Normally a day like this would have cheered her, especially if she had spent it with Paul, drinking hot chocolate and cuddling.

"Hey, you!" came a cheerful voice.

Ginny appeared in the doorway wearing a pale blue smock Bess had seen on some of the hospital staff.

"Are you a doctor already?" Bess asked, smiling weakly. "I knew you were smart, but—"

"I started my volunteer work this week," Ginny explained, relieved to see Bess joking.

"Great," Bess replied. This was the first time Bess had seen Ginny since the accident, and she knew Ginny would want to say how sorry she was. But bracing herself, Bess didn't think she could take another tearful scene.

Ginny must have read her mind. "So the food's not so hot," she said, nodding at Bess's full tray.

"Does your volunteer work include kitchen duty?" Bess asked hopefully.

"Sorry." Ginny shrugged and lowered herself onto the edge of the bed to give Bess's knee a squeeze. "The vigil was really beautiful, Bess," she said. "There were so many people. Do you want me to tell you about it?" she asked gingerly.

"I'm glad a lot of people went," Bess replied, "and that it was beautiful, but maybe later. Do you mind?"

Getting up, Ginny gave her a cheerful smile. "Absolutely not. I have to get down to Pediatrics to observe a procedure anyway. I just stopped in to say hello. I can visit any time now, you know. I'll come back soon."

Everyone seems so busy, Bess thought to herself as Ginny closed the door. Except me. I don't even have Glasseburg's acting class to look forward to anymore.

Just then the door opened. Bess turned her head, not in the mood to play hostess.

"Bess?"

"Nancy!" Bess breathed, relieved. Nancy she'd see anytime. "George!" Her two best friends. "Sit down here," she said, patting the bed. "I have something I want to tell you."

She saw Nancy and George exchange glances.

"After I get out of here, I'm going home to River Heights for a while," Bess began, figuring she should share her news.

Nancy nodded. "The doctors want you to recuperate. They told us."

"You need lots of rest," George added.

"But I want you to know, because you've always been my best friends on the planet"—Bess paused to catch her breath—"I want you know that even when I recover, I'm not sure I'm going to come back to Wilder."

Casey was sitting at a picnic table at Adventure World, an outdoor action center a half hour outside of Weston. While Zach was buying lunch at the concession stand, she listened to the screams and shouts from the direction of the giant roller coaster. The huge bungee-jumping tower loomed above her, casting a shadow across the entire park.

Casey hadn't thought too much about the jump. She was more into the idea of a day with Zach in the sunshine. But now that she was here, she couldn't even bring herself to look up at the little platform at the top of the tower.

I must be out of my mind, Casey thought to

herself. I have an opening-night performance in a few hours, and I'm about to tie a big rubber band around my ankle and jump off a ten-story building?

But something else was tugging at her, too—something deeper—the picture of Charley at home in L.A. If he could see her now . . . with Zach.

This, she thought, is just what he was talking about when he proposed. When he went on and on about the temptations facing a beautiful woman surrounded by intelligent, good-looking men.

Zach is just a friend, she reminded herself. Still, she knew Charley would hit the roof.

"Wow, it's amazing how much you miss American food when you're traveling!" Zach said, returning with a tray of fast food. He eagerly squeezed thick lines of ketchup and mustard on his hot dog.

"Hot dogs aren't international?" Casey asked.

"Not in Nepal," Zach said breezily.

"Nepal?" Casey asked.

"Or Australia."

"Must have been rough," Casey muttered.

Zach flashed a pearly smile, which, set off against his tan, was almost blinding. "Oh, it was. I lived in a tent in a surfers' hangout on the Queensland coast for three months. Sand, crystal water, tropical fish, sunshine. But trekking in

Nepal was the highlight. That was six months ago—I think." He laughed. "I kind of lost track."

"How long were you gone?" Casey asked.

"Just a year," Zach replied easily.

Well, he's anything but dull, Casey told herself. Why does he have to be so good-looking? While Zach polished off his hot dog, Casey thought about how mundane and average her life seemed, compared to his. Even Charley didn't really measure up on the exhilaration scale.

I never thought I'd meet someone who made TV stardom seem so dull, she thought. She wondered whether she'd trade her fame and money for a year of traveling around the world, and thought she might.

Zach popped the last french fry in his mouth and gave his stomach a slap. *"Now* I'm ready. What do you say?"

Casey looked down at her empty plate. "You want me to jump after eating all *this?"* she asked.

"Food makes you brave," Zach recited.

Casey eyed first him, then the tower warily.

I'm sick just thinking about it, she decided.

Zach fished out a few loose bills from his pocket for the jumping fees. After counting them, he reached back in his pocket.

"Got enough?" Casey asked.

"Plenty," Zach insisted. He took out a wallet, opened it, and added more bills to his pile.

As Zach counted the bills, he left his wallet

lying open. Inside, sheathed in plastic, was a photograph of a young girl with long blond hair.

Casey looked at it and smiled. "Your sister?" She nodded at the wallet.

Zach blinked, hesitated, then grinned. "Yep," he said casually, snapping the wallet closed. He slipped it back into his fanny pack, then peered up at the tower.

"So here we go," he said, staring at Casey, his eyes glinting ominously. He stood up and waited for her.

But Casey didn't budge. She felt a wave of fear and nausea in her stomach. Or was it just the hot dogs? Whatever, she would take it as a sign.

"Uh . . . I don't think so," she said, smiling guiltily. "But I'd love to watch."

Nancy opened the door to her room and sighed with relief when she found it empty.

Always talkative and cheerful, Kara was not the person Nancy wanted to see right then. She still felt strange after her visit with Bess. For the first time, she'd been unable to help her friend. George had felt the same way. Nancy wondered if Paul's death was the worst thing that had ever happened to the three of them.

"It might be," she murmured out loud, lowering herself onto the edge of her bed. She had one more difficult job to do: call Ned.

Checking her watch, she realized she had to

hurry. She was meeting Jake at Anthony's for an early supper before the one-acts.

As she dialed Ned's phone number, Nancy felt a wave of memories wash over her. Even after going out with Jake all this time, she still knew Ned's number at Emerson College by heart. She'd dialed it hundreds of times from her home in River Heights while she and Ned had kept up their long-distance relationship. A small smile came to her lips as she remembered all those conversations. All those times she'd told him she loved him.

And when the phone was picked up on the other end and Ned's familiar voice said hello, Nancy leaned back against the wall, relieved. In the shadow of Bess's pain, she needed to reach out to old friends.

"Guess who," she said.

After a slight pause, Ned replied, "I don't have to guess. How are you, Nan?"

"How are *you?*" she quickly said. She didn't want her news to be the first thing they talked about. "How are classes? How is your, um, friend?"

Nancy rolled her eyes, chiding herself. Ned had started seeing someone new after they'd broken up, and she still didn't know how to talk about it. But Ned made it easy: "Fine," he said happily. "Everything's fine. Working too hard—"

"You always did."

Ned laughed. "And my *friend,*" he said, "isn't *that* kind of friend anymore. We're just regular friends now—if you know what I mean."

Nancy chuckled. "I guess we know each other too well to talk in code, huh?"

"I guess we do," Ned replied, and paused. "It's good to hear your voice. So what's up? Sounds like you have something on your mind."

"You can still read me like an open book," Nancy said affectionately. "You're right, but it isn't good news. It's about Bess."

"Is she okay?"

"Not exactly. She's in the hospital."

"What happened?" Ned asked.

"She was in an accident. She's going to be all right, though," Nancy added quickly. "She'll probably have to go home for a while to recuperate. She was riding a motorcycle with her boyfriend when a car hit them."

"That's terrible," Ned said. "What about her boyfriend?"

"His name is . . . was, Paul Cody. He was killed."

At first Ned didn't reply. Nancy couldn't even hear him breathing. "Ned, you still there?"

"That's really awful," he finally answered. "I don't know what to say. I'll call Bess."

Nancy nodded—as if Ned could see her. "I think she'd like that. She needs all the support she can get. She really loved him."

"Poor Bess," Ned said softly. "It's hard to imagine how anyone could deal with that."

"Bess is strong," Nancy assured him.

"And he was your friend, too," Ned added. "How are you?"

"I'll be okay. I'm too concerned about Bess right now. I'm not really thinking of myself."

"Well, you should," Ned said firmly.

Nancy glanced at her desk, where she'd once put Ned's picture. But that was when she first got to Wilder. She wished she could see his face now, though. You always say the right things, Nancy said to him in her mind.

"What worries me is that Bess is talking about not coming back to school," Nancy said. "She thinks it might be too painful and that she wouldn't be able to concentrate on classes."

"It'll take time, but she'll come around," Ned said. "She'll be back. She'll need all of her friends around her, though."

"We'll be here."

"So will I," Ned replied. "In fact I'll call her right now. What's her number at the hospital?"

Nancy gave Ned the number. "Stay in touch, okay?" she said.

"Count on it," Ned replied. "We have to stick together. We're all good friends. That will never change, Nancy."

We are good friends, Nancy thought as she put down the phone. We definitely are.

"There," the makeup artist from Natural Shades Cosmetics said as she finally released the eyelash curler and stepped away.

Ouch, Pam wanted to reply. Would she have to go through this every day? The moment of truth, she thought, raising her eyes to the mirror.

"Whoa!" Pam burst out laughing. "What is that?"

"*That* is a phenomenal makeup job," the makeup woman said. "I take it you've never seen one before."

"Thanks for the compliment, I guess," Pam muttered, looking at the stranger in the mirror.

"And a good-looking girl beneath it," the woman conceded. "I'll go get Mr. Potter."

It was strange to see herself all made up, Pam realized, still captivated by her reflection. She almost couldn't tell if she looked pretty or not.

But after a few minutes Pam decided it was too weird to sit and stare at her new face, so she got up and wandered around the room. She went to the door and poked her head into the hallway, wondering if she could spot Reva or anyone else she knew.

Just then a girl came out of one of the other rooms and started walking down the hallway in Pam's direction. When Pam saw her, she almost gasped. The other girl was made up exactly like Pam. But she was so beautiful she didn't even look human. It was Tamara, the one Reva had pointed out the day before.

Great, Pam thought sadly, watching Tamara stroll down the hall, I don't stand a chance against her. She walked back to the mirror and dropped glumly into her chair.

"Hey, what's the frown for?" Jesse asked as he poked his head through the doorway. "The look is naturally beautiful," he teased, "not naturally unhappy."

"Sorry." Pam grinned.

"Wow!" Jesse said as he came closer. "You look fantastic!"

"Really?" Pam asked. She glanced back at the mirror. "I hardly recognize myself," she admitted.

"Well, the products suit you," Jesse said. "And the camera will love you."

"You think so?" Pam felt her spirits rise.

"I know so," Jesse said, giving her an appraising look. "Remember, I look at women for a living. And you're definitely a beautiful woman."

"Thanks," Pam said. She was starting to feel less self-conscious about so many compliments.

"You look as if you don't believe me, Miss Miller," Jesse said, clucking his tongue. "Well, the camera never lies," he said, pulling a photo out of his folder and picking up a hand mirror.

He stepped behind her chair and bent down. Then he reached around her shoulders, holding up a photo from yesterday's shoot and the mirror for her to compare it to her made-up face.

"Wow!" Pam said as she looked at the photo. She had to admit she looked great, and she was filled with a rush of pride and excitement.

"This photo is beautiful," she whispered, before she could stop herself.

"It's not the picture that's beautiful, Pam," Jesse said. "I told you Richard knew how to shoot beautiful women, didn't I?" Jesse asked, his breath fanning across Pam's cheek.

"You did," Pam admitted.

"That was how great you looked without makeup," Jesse said, shaking the photo. "Now just imagine that face looking even sexier."

Pam was so flustered she had to drop her eyes. She knew she was blushing.

"That boyfriend of yours must not be telling you often enough how gorgeous you are," Jesse said. "I don't think he's doing his job."

"And I don't think this is part of yours," a deep male voice said from behind them.

Pam raised her eyes to the mirror and saw the figure standing behind her. It was Jamal, glaring at the image of her with Jesse's arms draped over her shoulders.

Nancy was grabbing her coat when she heard a knock on the suite door.

"Anyone else here?" she called out as she made her way back to the lounge. "I guess not," she muttered, reaching for the door.

"Anna!" Nancy cried. Anna Pederson stood in the doorway, a backpack slung over her shoulder and a forlorn expression on her face. "Does your foster family know where you are?" Nancy asked, ushering the girl inside.

Anna shook her head.

"Do they even know you're gone?" Nancy asked.

"I told them I was going to the mall," Anna admitted. "But I just had to see you, so I took the bus up here. Did you find out anything about my dad?" she asked. "Can you help him?"

"I don't know," Nancy said. "I can't promise anything. You shouldn't get your hopes up."

"You couldn't find the guy who was in the car with him?" Anna asked.

Nancy wondered if she should tell Anna about Ryan. But one look at the girl's worried face and Nancy knew she had to give her some hope, slim as it was.

"I got a description of a guy who was in the bar that night," Nancy explained. "He left when your dad did. And today I ran into this same guy. He had a book of matches like the ones the police found in your father's car."

"He must be the one, then," Anna cried. "Did you call the police? Will they let my dad out now?"

"We don't have enough evidence, Anna," Nancy replied. "Maybe this guy gave the matches to your dad while they were in the bar. We can't prove he was in the car with your dad or that he was driving."

"Well, can I look at the car myself?" Anna asked. "Maybe the police missed something."

She's so desperate, Nancy thought. And I promised her I'd do everything I could to help.

"Look," Nancy said quickly, before she could change her mind. "I don't know if the police will let us look at the car.—"

"But can't we try?" Anna begged.

"I'll drive you to the impound lot," Nancy agreed, "and we'll ask to see the car. But after that, I've got to take you back to your foster home. Getting yourself in trouble won't help your dad."

CHAPTER 10

I can't believe you embarrassed me again!" Pam shouted at Jamal as she stormed away from the alliance center. "How old do you think you are, anyway? I *thought* you were in college. I *thought* you were more mature than that!"

Pam had never felt more embarrassed in her life. Except maybe the last time Jamal had acted this way—the day before.

"Is this going to be a habit with you?" Pam demanded, spinning around to confront him. "Who is this macho caveman jerk my boyfriend has become? Because I don't want him."

"Hold on, hold on. I wasn't barging in on you," Jamal argued. "At least I didn't mean to. I said I'd help post flyers for the alliance center lecture series, and I thought the flyers were in that room.

Nobody told me that Natural Shades was using it." Jamal reached out to touch Pam on the arm. "But I'm not sorry I *did* walk in on you, because I got there just in time."

"In time to do what?" Pam asked exasperated. "Totally embarrass me? Ruin any chance I might have had of being picked as one of the Natural Shades models?"

"No," Jamal said defensively. "To stop that creep Jesse."

"Stop him from doing what, Jamal?" Pam asked. "From doing his job?" Pam rolled her eyes. She felt as if she were talking to a child.

"Well, I guess you just didn't think what he was doing was a problem," Jamal said moodily. "Maybe you enjoyed having another man's arms around you."

"I can't believe you just said that." Pam shook her head at him. "Who do you think I am, anyway?"

"I'm sorry," Jamal replied quickly. "You know I didn't mean that. I'm just upset. I know it was nothing to you," he allowed. "But it was more than business for him, I could tell. Trust me on that, Pam."

Suddenly Pam stopped in her tracks. "That's just it," she realized. "You always say 'Trust me.' *You* know what I want. *You* know what I think. *You* know what I should do."

Pam shook her head and looked at Jamal. "Just because I don't want you to run my life, you think I don't trust you. But you've got it all wrong, don't you see? This is not about me trusting you. It's about *you* trusting *me.*" Pam blinked back the tears she felt forming.

"No," Jamal said, stepping toward her. "That's not true. Of course I do—"

"You don't," Pam cut him off. "You don't trust me to know when I'm hungry or when I should study and when I shouldn't. To know what I think about things. To know what interests me." Pam paused. "And you don't trust me when I'm around other men."

"But it's not you I don't trust," Jamal said. "It's them."

"Forget them!" Pam cried, surprising herself. "Let me tell you this one more time, and, Jamal Lewis, you'd better listen. *I'm* in this model contest because *I* want to be. Because it's fun and exciting. Nothing is happening between me and Jesse Potter. He was just showing me a photograph of myself so that I could see how different I looked after the makeover and so I could believe that maybe, just maybe, my chances of winning aren't so impossible."

Pam sighed and looked at her boyfriend. She had never been so upset with Jamal. It was almost as if they didn't know each other.

"Give me a little credit, will you?" Pam added. "Jesse's not interested in me romantically. And even if he was," Pam said, holding up her hand to keep Jamal quiet as he started to interrupt, "don't you think I can handle myself? Do you think I'm totally stupid? That I don't know how to say no to an unwanted pass?"

"Of course you're not stupid," Jamal replied softly.

"And I can take care of myself?" Pam pressed.

Jamal opened his mouth, but nothing came out.

"Jamal!" Pam cried.

"But I don't want you to *have* to take care of yourself," Jamal finally said. He took a step toward her. "*I* want to take care of you."

Pam sighed. Jamal looked so hurt and sincere. Finally she couldn't help it—she burst out laughing.

"What?" Jamal asked. "Are you laughing at me?"

"Of course I'm not laughing *at* you," Pam said. Grabbing Jamal's hand, she pulled him over to her. "I'm laughing at this whole situation. Don't you see? It's like a bad movie. Every time this guy stepped *near* me, you happened to be walking by."

"Luckily," Jamal muttered.

"No," Pam corrected him. "Bad-luckily. Stupidly. Totally ridiculously. I turn around and there's your scowling face, but nothing was going on between Jesse and me." Pam paused and then asked, "How long have we been together, Jamal?"

He caught her eye. "Forever?" he whispered.

Pam grinned back. "Feels like it sometimes,

doesn't it? And how long are we going to stay together?"

"Longer than forever," Jamal replied, smiling back at her.

"So why are we fighting about this?" Pam asked.

"Because I care about you," Jamal said. "And I'm a jealous idiot sometimes."

"As long as you can admit it," Pam replied, "you can always be my idiot."

"This isn't the same without Bess," Casey whispered as she and Brian made their way through Hewlitt Center to the dressing rooms. It was opening night for the one-act plays, but Casey wasn't thinking about her performance. "Bess rehearsed hard, and the performance meant so much to her. She should be here, Brian. And Paul—"

"I know," Brian said, putting his arm around her. "His death seems unreal to me, even though I know it actually happened. I don't think I'm really dealing with it yet. But we've still got to get through tonight."

"I know. I'll get myself together," Casey said, shaking her head. "It's just so unfair, and I feel so helpless. I wish we could do something."

"Wait," Brian said, pointing to the stage door. "There's Jeanne Glasseburg with Alan."

"Do you think she knows about Bess?" Casey asked. "Maybe she doesn't. We've got to tell her what happened. This was supposed to be Bess's one chance, and she's going to miss it."

"Jeanne *was* expecting to see Bess," Brian agreed. "I'm sure she'll wonder what happened to her."

"It would be terrible if she thought Bess couldn't handle the pressure or something," Casey added. "We have to make sure she knows the truth."

"Okay," Brian said, taking a deep breath. "You're right. Let's tell her."

"Great." Casey grinned. "I love a good cause."

Casey pushed Brian ahead of her until they were standing right next to Professor Farber and Jeanne Glasseburg. After a moment the two adults noticed them and paused in their discussion.

"Excuse us, Ms. Glasseburg," Brian said. "But we had to tell you that our friend Bess Marvin can't be in the production tonight."

"What happened?" Ms. Glasseburg asked.

Professor Farber nodded. "Bess was involved in a terrible accident a few nights ago."

"You remember Bess, don't you?" Casey asked Ms. Glasseburg. "You stopped by our table the other night to speak to her."

"Of course I remember her," Ms. Glasseburg said, turning back to Alan. "The delightful young blond woman who did the funny improv, right? She was in an accident?"

"A motorcycle accident," Casey explained. "She's in the hospital."

"I'm sorry to hear that," Ms. Glasseburg said. "I was looking forward to her performance."

"Exactly," Brian said quickly. "That's what we wanted to ask you about. I mean, considering what happened to her, and to her boyfriend . . ." Brian trailed off.

"He was killed." Casey picked up where Brian left off. "And Bess is lucky to be alive. I know it's going to be hard for her to get over her loss, and she was really looking forward to being in your class."

"Well, I'm flattered to hear that," Ms. Glasseburg said. "And I'm truly sorry for your friend. But it is an invitational class. If you're asking me to include her in my group to make up for the shock of losing her boyfriend, I'm afraid—"

"No, no," Casey interrupted. "We didn't mean that. It's just that everyone knows that tonight's performances are also an audition for you. And since Bess can't be here, she'll miss not only the performance, but also her chance to audition for you."

"We thought maybe you could let Bess audition for you later," Brian said. "You know, after she's out of the hospital."

"Oh, I see," Ms. Glasseburg said, nodding. "I am very sorry to hear this news. I do remember her, but still, I just don't know if I can arrange something like that. Tonight was really to help me judge everyone against the same standard. You've all had the same preparation time, you're all working under the same pressures, and you'll perform before the same audience . . ."

"Please, just think about it," Casey begged.

"I can't promise anything," Ms. Glasseburg said carefully. "But I'll consider it."

"Thank you," Casey smiled, and Brian took her arm and pulled her away.

"I hope we didn't go overboard," Brian whispered.

"Well, we did what we could," Casey replied as they made their way back to the dressing rooms. "And at least she said she'd think about it."

"But we can't tell Bess what we did," Brian warned. "Not unless Jeanne Glasseburg gives her another chance to audition."

Casey crossed her fingers. "I just hope we can bring her some good news. It wouldn't be fair for her to lose everything."

When Ginny left the hospital after a long day of volunteering, she was on cloud nine. The work had been more inspiring than she'd imagined it could be. Not only was she awed and inspired by working with the doctors and nurses in the pediatric ward, but she had observed her first operation. Ginny had sat in the visitors' area above the operating theater to watch a very delicate and unusual heart bypass operation on a three-year-old girl.

Ginny was bursting to talk about her day. Without even thinking about it, she headed for Ray's dorm.

But would he really want to hear about this? Ginny wondered, slowing down. And more important, would he even listen?

After their argument the night before, Ginny wasn't sure. She cringed when she recalled some of the things they'd said to each other. She knew Ray was under a lot of pressure, but she still wasn't sure she was ready to forgive him. And she definitely wasn't up for another fight. Ginny turned toward Thayer Hall instead.

If I can't talk to Ray, I'll have to find someone else to talk to.

Her stomach rumbled in response, and Ginny remembered that she hadn't eaten anything all day. She'd been so caught up in her work at the hospital that she hadn't taken a break. She decided to stop by the Hot Truck on her way back to her dorm and fortify herself with a sandwich.

The crowd at the Hot Truck was small, and when Ginny saw one guy placing his order, she grinned in delight.

"It's good to see a familiar face," Ginny said, walking over to him. "I hate having to wait out here by myself."

"Look who's here," Frank Chung said, pleasantly surprised. "How are you doing, Ginny? How are your parents?"

"They're great," she replied. "Thanks for asking."

Frank was a fine arts major who had helped Ginny out of an awkward situation when her parents had come to Wilder for a visit and she'd tried to introduce them to her rocker boyfriend, Ray. Since then, Ginny and Frank had become good friends.

"I heard about the Beat Poets' Pacific Records deal," Frank added. "It's all over the Wilder radio station. That's fantastic. Ray must be out of his mind."

"Yeah," Ginny said. "Unfortunately, he's driving me a little crazy, too."

"Really?" Frank asked, concerned. "I don't mean to pry, but if you want to talk about it, I'm here to listen. Hey, weren't you thinking of getting off the med school track?" Frank asked.

"For a while I was," Ginny said. "But now I don't know anymore."

"Which means?" Frank asked.

"I might want to go to medical school after all. I actually feel a little guilty not talking to Ray about this," Ginny admitted. "But he hasn't been able to talk about anything but the record deal, and I wasn't up to having another fight."

"It's okay," Frank said. "Sometimes we all need an unbiased opinion."

"The thing is that my parents want me to be a doctor," Ginny said. "They're nervous about my relationship with Ray, and they disapprove of his music and my writing songs with him. But it's really been great for me. I never knew I had a creative side."

"And they're sure that if you don't become a doctor, it'll be because of Ray's influence," Frank finished.

"Exactly," Ginny said. "Which really bothers me. But now that I've started working at the hospital, I'm beginning to realize I actually *do* want to be a doctor."

"So why the unhappy face?" Frank asked.

"Because my parents won't ever believe it was my *own* decision," Ginny explained.

"I see." Frank nodded. "You want them to understand that you aren't going to be a doctor just to please them. You want them to be happy for you because you're happy for yourself, right?"

"Exactly," Ginny said, overwhelmed at how Frank had managed to express her thoughts so perfectly. "But now Ray thinks I'm copping out of a more creative life. I don't think he believes I can make up my own mind. And I don't think he'll ever believe I want to become a doctor for my own reasons, and not just to please my parents."

"I'm sure he just doesn't want you to sell yourself short," Frank replied. "He wants to make sure you're happy."

"I guess." Ginny sighed. "It's pretty frustrating trying to live up to everyone's expectations."

"Just don't lose sight of what you really want," Frank said. "Follow that, and everyone else will come around in time. My parents did." He chuckled. "They had my whole life mapped out for me, including the girl I would marry, the house I would live in, and names for all of the kids I would have."

"Are you serious?" Ginny cried. "That sounds terrible."

Frank laughed. "Well, it wasn't that bad," he admitted. "I'm exaggerating, but now maybe things don't look so bad, right?"

That was true, Ginny realized. She already felt much better about her decision to be a doctor. It was a relief to talk with someone who could understand how she was feeling.

But, Ginny wondered anxiously, would Ray understand, too?

CHAPTER 11

"This is a madhouse," Jake said, sheltering Nancy in the circle of his arms in the backstage crush after the opening-night performance of the one-act plays. "But I'll take any opportunity I can to get close to you," he added, squeezing her lovingly.

"That's the only reason I don't mind the crush," Nancy agreed, smiling up at him as she and Jake were jostled by crew members and actors. "In fact, I'd be happy to get out of here and be crushed by you alone somewhere."

"Great idea," Jake murmured happily.

"But," Nancy said, "first we have to find Casey and Brian and congratulate them."

Even though it had been hard to watch the plays without Bess, Nancy thought they'd turned out great. Nancy did find herself thinking about Bess often, but she was still able to enjoy the show.

Getting near her friends was impossible. Casey and Brian were at the center of a crush of people, and Nancy didn't relish a wrestling match. Casey finally glanced up and spotted them.

"You were great!" Nancy and Jake cried together as Casey and Brian waved hello and yelled out their thanks.

"Good," Jake muttered, yanking Nancy away. "We've done our duty. Now let's get to the me-crushing-you-in-a-nice-dark-place part."

"Your apartment?" Nancy teased.

"I wish," Jake said. "But we're meeting everyone at the Underground. Unless you don't want to go?"

"No, that sounds like fun," Nancy said. "And it'll be dark enough to sneak in a few kisses."

"I'm hoping," Jake said as he led Nancy toward the exit.

"Wait." Nancy grabbed Jake's arm as they passed through the stage wing. "There's the guy I told you about."

Ryan was standing beside one of the curtains, rolling up electrical wires.

"What do you want to do?" Jake asked.

When Ryan glanced up and saw Nancy staring at him, his eyes narrowed.

"I'm not going to let him off this time," Nancy

answered, pulling Jake with her. "I want some answers."

As soon as he saw her starting toward him, Ryan dropped the wires he was working on and sighed.

"Hey, Ryan," Nancy said boldly. "Do you have a minute?"

"I'm busy," he said uncomfortably.

"This won't take long," Nancy replied. "Let me tell you what's going on," she explained. "A girl's father is in jail for a hit-and-run accident that happened two nights ago."

"The motorcycle accident?" Ryan asked, surprised. "But why would I have anything to do with that?"

"I know you were at Blake's Place on Thursday night," Nancy said. "The bartender there described you and said you left the bar at the same time as the driver of the hit-and-run car. The driver insists that out in the parking lot someone asked him for a ride. That someone could have been you."

"What?" Ryan asked in shock. "Are you joking?"

"My best friend was hurt in the accident, and her boyfriend was killed," Nancy said soberly. "This is no joke."

"You know Bess?" he asked. "Well, I know her, too, and I'm really sorry she was hurt, but I didn't have anything to do with that accident."

"Maybe you can tell us where you went when you left the bar," Jake suggested.

"No way," Ryan snapped, staring at them both, his mouth a grim line.

"I'm going to tell the police what I know," Nancy finally said. "They'll probably call you in for questioning. I'm sure the bartender will pick you out of a lineup. I guess it's your choice whether you want to cooperate with me or not."

Nancy turned away, disappointed. She'd hoped her last comment would make Ryan nervous enough to talk to her.

"Hold on," Ryan called out sharply from behind her. "You've got it all wrong."

Ryan glanced around him and then motioned Nancy and Jake to step back against the wall, out of the way of people milling around backstage.

"I was in Blake's Place on Thursday night," Ryan admitted quietly. "And I left at the same time as that really drunk guy. He's the one the police are holding, right?"

Nancy nodded. "His name is Pederson."

"Okay. But *I* didn't drive him home," Ryan said sharply. "There was someone else in the parking lot. A young guy, tall, with dark hair. He was talking to Pederson when I left."

"That's convenient," Jake commented.

"Maybe," Ryan said, "but it's also true."

"Yesterday I noticed you had a book of matches from a place called the Back Porch,"

Nancy pressed. "The police found a book of those matches in Mr. Pederson's car."

"And *he* doesn't smoke," Jake added.

"I'm not the only person in the world who still smokes," Ryan replied. "I saw the matches lying on the bar at Blake's Place. So I took them," Ryan said defensively. "That's not exactly a crime, is it?"

"But if you had nothing to do with the accident, why were you so nervous when I tried to talk to you yesterday?" Nancy challenged. "Didn't you realize how suspicious your behavior would seem?"

"There's a reason I didn't want to answer your questions," Ryan said angrily, his voice frustrated and low. "I went to Blake's to meet a woman friend of mine. A *married* woman friend." Ryan sighed. "Get it? And I'd really like to keep that meeting quiet."

Well, Nancy thought, Ryan's involvement in an affair would certainly explain his suspicious behavior. But if there really was someone else in the car with Mr. Pederson, how could they ever find him now? They had almost nothing to go on.

"Look, I'm really sorry about your friend," Ryan added. "But I'm not the person you're looking for. If the police want to take my fingerprints, they're welcome. They won't find them anywhere in that car," he said, his voice full of calm conviction.

"Okay." Nancy sighed. "Thanks for talking to

us. I don't think you'll have to worry about your married friend getting involved."

"Wait a minute!" Ryan called, before Nancy and Jake had gone more than a few steps. "I just remembered something. Maybe it'll help. The guy in the parking lot had a bag with him. Like a duffel or something, on his shoulder."

"Thanks," Nancy said, summoning a smile.

Ryan shrugged and turned backstage.

"What do you think?" Jake asked, taking Nancy by the arm and steering her to the exit.

"I don't know," Nancy admitted. "I get the feeling he's telling the truth. But that just means we're back to square one."

Beside Bess's hospital bed was a growing heap of pink tissues, and another untouched tray of food. The TV above her was playing something, but she had no idea what, even though she'd been staring at it for hours. All she could see was the never-ending movie playing in her head: Paul's face, the accident, Paul's face, the accident, over and over and over. She didn't even know what time it was.

She thought of her future, recuperating in River Heights, in her room and her bed, surrounded by the things she grew up with. But instead of relief she felt sadness. She was caught. She knew she'd be sad here at Wilder, where she'd be reminded of Paul everywhere she went. But she'd be sad at home, too. That's where her old life was. Her high school life. Life before Paul. That wasn't her anymore.

Do I want to go backward? she thought. Obviously the answer was no. But a future on campus without Paul just seemed too painful to endure.

Suddenly she heard a commotion outside her door. "I know visiting hours are over," a familiar high-pitched voice was saying, "but we'll only stay two minutes, we promise!"

The door burst open, and some of Bess's Kappa sisters, including Eileen, Holly Thornton, and even Soozie Beckerman, were standing there holding two huge bouquets and a fruit basket.

"Ta-da!" Holly said dramatically.

Bess managed a strained smile. "It's great to see you guys. What time is it? Did the nurses give you a hard time about coming to see me?"

Eileen blew on her fingers. "Nothing we couldn't handle," she said with a wink. "It's Saturday night, and we were just thinking: Bess shouldn't be alone on Saturday night."

"No way," Soozie chimed in.

Bess looked at her quizzically. She and Soozie hadn't exactly had the best relationship. Soozie was a temperamental, self-centered, nasty schemer, especially when it came to Bess. And Soozie and Holly seemed to be locked in a constant struggle for power in the Kappa house.

But here she was. Which Bess thought was nice, if not curious. Maybe Soozie wasn't as self-absorbed as everyone thought. Or maybe she'd called a temporary truce.

"Saturday night," Bess said. "This was opening night for the one-acts! How'd they go?"

Holly gave a double thumbs-up. "Great." Suddenly her expression drooped. "But they really missed you."

"I'm sure," Bess murmured.

"No, really," Soozie insisted, obviously struggling to find something nice to say. "I was, um, really looking forward to seeing you."

Bess gave her a crooked smile. "Thanks."

Cradling the fruit basket, Eileen moved closer to the bed. "Here," she said, holding out the basket.

"Gee, thanks," Bess said halfheartedly. "Fruit."

Eileen rolled her eyes. "Not just fruit, dummy. Take a closer look."

Holly walked over and picked up a banana and an orange. Mixed in with the fruit lay a dozen assorted candy bars.

"Hospital food is always terrible," Holly said, eyeing Bess's untouched tray. "We wanted to bring you something really nutritious."

Bess felt something foreign and uncomfortable on her face: a real smile, her first one since Thursday. She was laughing softly. "Thanks," she said.

Suddenly, though, a wave of fatigue swept over her.

"Whup, she's tired," Eileen blurted. "I'd recognize that expression anywhere. You're not in a hospital for nothing, you know."

Bess nodded. "Thanks for coming, guys. You really cheered me up."

On their way out, Holly turned and gave her a little wave, her expression serious, concerned. "Feel better," she mouthed.

"I'm glad you came," Bess replied.

The door closed. Exhausted from a long day with many visitors, Bess aimed the remote at the TV and flipped it off. But just as she reached for the light, the phone rang.

At first she just looked at it. She didn't think she could take another consoling conversation. But it was late, so whoever was calling really wanted to talk to her. "Hello?" she said.

She heard commotion and laughter on the other end. "Bess, it's Brian!"

"Brian," she said. "I heard everything went great."

"It *did*. Sorry I'm shouting, but I'm at the cast party and it's really loud! Everyone here wants you to know how much we missed you tonight. We can't wait for you to come back and blow everyone in the drama department away! Can you hear me?"

"I hear you, Brian," Bess said as loud as she could.

"Bess, I can't really understand you," he said

over the noise. "But I'll call you tomorrow, okay? Everyone here loves and misses you. 'Bye!"

Boy, when you're in the hospital, you really learn who your friends are. Bess smiled as she put down the phone.

As she drifted off to sleep, Bess thought about how happy her friends seemed to be. They were so anxious to cheer her up and let her know she wasn't alone.

But their good wishes were having the opposite effect on her. Their reaching out was making Bess want to run away. Other people's happiness just reminded her of her own unhappiness. And everyone else's company reinforced her own loneliness. She loved Nancy and George. She loved all of her friends. But none of them was Paul. The others, as much as they tried, would never be able to replace him.

Bess drifted off to sleep with one quick thought: I have to leave Wilder.

As the guitar player on the small stage at the Underground strummed one of George's favorite songs, she leaned against Will and draped an arm around his muscular back. Nancy and Jake sat across the candlelit table. The other tables were packed, and people lined the walls, listening intently. They were quiet, soaking up the mellow atmosphere, sipping at their drinks.

"This music is perfect," George said. "It's good

to relax for a while, isn't it?" George asked, leaning over to give Will a quick kiss on the neck.

"It is," he agreed softly, putting his warm hand on her knee. "Thanks."

"It's been a long day," Nancy said.

A waitress came with their order: large fries, onion rings, and sodas all around.

"Hey, was that guy you were talking to backstage the same one you tried to talk to in Java Joe's this morning?" George asked Nancy between bites.

Nancy and Jake nodded.

"Did he tell you anything more this time?"

Nancy put down her soda. "I did find out why he was acting so suspicious," Nancy explained. "He said he went to Blake's Place to meet a married woman. He was afraid that if he got involved in the accident investigation, he'd have to identify her."

"I guess that's a good reason to act suspicious," Will threw in sardonically.

"But he did say there was somebody else in the parking lot that night," Jake added.

"Really?" George said. "So somebody else was driving the car?"

Nancy shrugged. "Maybe, but I don't know how we're going to find him. This guy didn't see the man clearly, so we don't have a detailed description to go on. All we know is that he was wearing a pair of unusual sunglasses."

George and Will exchanged puzzled looks. "What kind of sunglasses?" George asked.

"I'm not positive, but listen to this. I was out with Anna today," Nancy began, "and we swung by the impound lot where they're keeping Mr. Pederson's car."

"You broke into the impound lot?" George asked incredulously.

Nancy laughed. "No, but Anna convinced the manager that she needed to see if some of her schoolbooks were inside her dad's car."

"She's quick," Jake said. "Reporter in the making."

"The manager only let us look through the windows," Nancy continued. "The car is still part of the ongoing criminal investigation, and we weren't allowed to touch anything. But I did see the dent on the front bumper and the black paint that was scraped off Will's motorcycle."

George felt Will take her hand and give it a squeeze. "And inside?"

"Coffee cups, doughnut wrappers," Nancy said. "We were about to take off when I spotted something."

George leaned forward. "What?"

Nancy sipped her soda. "A pair of sunglasses, partly hidden under the driver's seat."

Will shrugged. "So?"

"So they had oval lenses and wire rims—very cool." Nancy looked around the table. "Anna

143

said her father's sunglasses had heavy brown frames."

For a minute no one said a word. The soft strains of the guitar music hovered over them. But George's mind was racing. "This is another clue," she said, breaking the silence. "Someone else *was* in the car that night."

Everyone was nodding. "It sure seems that way," Nancy agreed.

George lifted her soda, deep in thought. As she drank, she suddenly noticed a familiar face across the room: Pam. She was sitting with Jamal at a corner table. George sensed that Pam had seen her, too, because she'd quickly turned away, her mouth pursed in a moody smirk.

"I'll be right back," George said with determination, pushing away from the table.

As she made her way across the room, George noticed that Pam looked especially stunning. Her face was subtly but skillfully made up so that her cheekbones seemed sharper and her eyes, enhanced by dark eye shadow, looked mysterious.

"Hi, guys," she said, kneeling down between them. "Remember me?"

Pam eyed her warily. "Maybe."

"Look," George said apologetically, "I was in a terrible mood last night. I'm sorry I was so sarcastic when you were on the phone with those Natural Shades people. It wasn't fair."

A light came to Pam's eyes, and her expression softened with relief.

Pam gave George's shoulder an affectionate squeeze. "I've been so busy that I haven't been much of a support team for you, but you know how much I care about Bess."

"I do," George replied. "It's difficult to find a way to help people in situations like this. So?" George prodded her teasingly. "How's it going with the contest, Miss Natural Shade? I have to say, you look *killer.*"

George noticed that Jamal frowned a little at her compliment to Pam.

But Pam leaned forward excitedly. "It's amazing. They gave me a makeover and took more photos. I think I really have a shot at being their model."

George nodded with pride. Then she winked at Jamal. "I'd keep an eye on her if I were you. At this rate she'll need a bodyguard soon."

"That's what I'm afraid of," Jamal muttered.

Pam shook her head. George saw her reach out and firmly take Jamal's hand. "He's having some trouble with the idea of strangers drooling over pictures of my gorgeous self," Pam said lightly.

"It's not strangers," Jamal said defensively. "Just that one guy—"

"But we've already talked this through," Pam interrupted, turning to him, though she was still talking to George. "Jamal *knows* he's the one I love."

If he didn't know before, George thought, he

does now. "He should be thanking his lucky stars," George replied, raising her brows at Jamal. "It's not every day an awesome girlfriend who's brainy and athletic also becomes a supermodel."

"I know!" Jamal finally blurted out. "So shoot me for worrying. I guess I'm not allowed to keep her a secret." He sighed, turning to smile at Pam. "And she does look amazing."

"I guess that's my cue to leave you two alone." George laughed. "I'm glad we spoke," she said to Pam. "I'm behind you one hundred percent."

"Thanks." Pam smiled and then elbowed Jamal in the side.

"Me, too," he moaned. "Me, too."

CHAPTER 12

Early Sunday morning Nancy made her way to the table Anna had picked for them at the Bumblebee Diner. Nancy had decided to take Anna out for breakfast. Knowing the girl was anxious, Nancy hated thinking of her in a foster home while her father was in jail.

"Anything new?" Anna asked the minute Nancy sat down.

"I saw that red-haired guy again," Nancy said with a sigh. "The one I mentioned yesterday."

"And he said he was there?" Anna held her breath.

"He was at Blake's Place," Nancy admitted, "but he wasn't driving your dad's car."

"Maybe that's what he said," Anna murmured, distressed, "but he could be lying, right?"

"He could be, but he has a pretty good alibi," Nancy replied.

"What is it?" Anna asked skeptically.

Nancy looked at her and smiled slightly. "Just trust me. I don't think he's guilty. But he did say he saw another guy in the parking lot that night."

"But how do you know he's not lying? I say we call the police right away," Anna blurted out. "Maybe the sunglasses are his. They could take this guy's fingerprints and match them and let my dad out of jail," she finished in a rush.

Nancy sighed as she looked at Anna's pained expression.

"I promise I'll tell the police everything I know," Nancy said. She put her hand on Anna's arm. "But I think Ryan was telling the truth. He seemed willing enough to have his fingerprints taken, and I don't think he was just bluffing."

"So what about this other guy, then?" Anna asked. "Are you going to talk to him?"

"That's the new problem," Nancy admitted. "We don't have a good description of him. All we know is that he's young and he had a bag with him."

"What kind of bag?" Anna asked. "We have to know. It's the only thing we have to go on, and maybe we can trace it."

"Maybe," Nancy said absently. But the bag wasn't really the only thing they had. They also had the sunglasses. Nancy knew she'd heard some comment about sunglasses recently, and she was racking her brain trying to remember when and where.

"Anna, are you sure those sunglasses don't belong to your dad?" Nancy asked again.

"I'm sure," Anna replied, sucking the whipped cream off the top of her cocoa. "I told you. They're definitely too cool for my dad. He wears this ugly brown pair, the kind that you can buy at the drugstore," Anna said, rolling her eyes. "The ones we saw in the car are the hip kind of sunglasses Kyle would wear." Kyle was a boy at school she had a crush on. "Because Kyle's, like, totally in fashion."

Suddenly an image of Zach Bainbridge flashed into Nancy's mind.

That's it! she remembered, snapping her fingers. Friday night Bill had told them how Zach's nickname in high school was the Star because he was always wearing sunglasses. And Bill had mentioned that Zach had lost his sunglasses recently.

Nancy's mind whirled. Was it possible . . . ?

Ryan had said the guy in the parking lot was young, which could mean he was about Zach's age. And Zach *had* arrived in Weston Thursday night. *And,* Nancy realized, her eyes widening, he was carrying a traveling bag.

It seemed crazy, Nancy realized. Bill Graham's high school buddy, a hit-and-run driver?

Nancy knew it was probably a long shot, but it wouldn't hurt to ask Zach questions.

"What is it?" Anna had noticed the intent expression on Nancy's face. "You look as if you know something."

Nancy shook her head. "It's only a hunch, but I just thought of someone who might be able to tell us something about the accident," she explained. "As soon as I drop you off, I'll try to find him."

"Drop me off?" Anna asked raising her eyes. "You *must* be kidding."

"Anna, I told your foster family I'd have you back by eleven," Nancy said, checking her watch.

"Nancy," Anna begged, "I don't care about my foster family. I care about my *father.* You have to let me go with you."

"Okay, okay," Nancy relented. "But don't get your hopes up too high."

On their way back from breakfast, Casey was giving Stephanie a blow-by-blow account of the cast party the night before when they ran into Zach outside Thayer Hall.

"Hey, ladies," Zach said, and grinned. "Are you telling Stephanie about all the fun she missed the other day at Adventure World?" he asked Casey, his eyes glinting merrily.

"Oh, yeah," Casey replied. "I filled her in."

"The part about her feeling sick just watching you bungee-jump was particularly compelling," Stephanie said. "I'm really sorry I missed it."

"So what's up?" Casey asked, noticing the bag on Zach's shoulder. "Are you leaving already?"

"You know me," Zach said. "I'm a traveling kind of guy."

"And the highlights in your hair are starting to fade," Stephanie teased, pointing at Zach's dark head. "Heading back to the beach?"

"Why?" he asked slyly, looking back and forth between them. "Care to join me?"

"Which one of us are you talking to?" Casey asked, pretending to be offended.

"Either," he said, leering. "But I'd prefer both."

"You *are* bad," Stephanie muttered.

"Actually, I'm on my way to the Underground to meet Bill and Dawn," Zach explained. "Then I'm going to hitch a ride back home."

"Isn't that dangerous?" Casey asked as Stephanie reached into her bag and fished out a cigarette.

"Are you going to nag me about smoking?" Stephanie moaned.

Casey laughed. "No, roomie. I meant the hitchhiking part. You think I care if you ruin your lungs?"

"Ahh, but you know how much I like danger," Zach replied, catching Casey's eye and winking. Then he turned to Stephanie. Please, allow me." Zach pulled a matchbook from his back pocket. "For old times' sake."

"So what do *I* get for old times' sake?" Casey asked with a fake pout. "A lukewarm hot dog?"

Zach turned and winked after he'd touched a match to Stephanie's cigarette. "How about another chance to jump with me?" he challenged.

"Thanks, but I'll stick with the memories," Casey muttered, shaking her head at the memory of Zach on his ten-story fall.

"Memories fade," Stephanie teased. "A jump stub would have been better."

"Since you missed your chance at a jump stub, you can have this," Zach said, pressing the matchbook into Stephanie's hand.

"Wow," Stephanie drawled, looking down at the black-and-orange cardboard square. "Last of the big spenders."

"Hey, come on," Zach replied. "You can't get them here in Weston."

Casey leaned over and read the name printed on the matchbook. "Hey, I know that place," she said. "The Back Porch is a club in L.A.

"All right, all right." Stephanie smiled. "In that case, we'll do you a favor." She pointed to his bag. "Why don't you leave that with us? We'll take it upstairs to the suite. Then you won't have to lug it around the restaurant."

"Thanks, ladies," Zach said, dropping his bag at their feet. "That means I can save our sweet goodbyes for later, right?"

"You're going to be late for lunch," Casey said, checking her watch.

"Okay, okay," Zach said. As he walked away, he turned and blew them a kiss.

"He's a looker," Casey admitted as she and Stephanie watched Zach disappear around the building. Then they looked at each other and burst out laughing.

"But I'm not sorry he's leaving," Casey admitted.

"I never thought I'd say this about a gorgeous guy," Stephanie agreed, "but he's trouble with a capital *T*."

"Too close for comfort, huh?" Casey said, raising an eyebrow at her flirtatious roommate. "I'm surprised you'd say that. Birds of a feather, you know . . ."

Stephanie snorted. "Excuse me. Zach is the come-on king. Even *I* can aspire to a bit more romance than that."

"Are you talking about Jonathan, by any chance?" Casey asked.

"I don't kiss and tell." Stephanie chuckled. "But give me some credit. I may surprise you," she said mysteriously. "Remember, I'm a working girl now. Maybe next semester I'll make the honor roll," she joked.

"Sure," Casey agreed. "Then you'll be elected president of your own sorority. You'll start wearing cashmere and pearls and going to bed at ten o'clock."

"You never know what changes a girl can make," Stephanie quipped. "Hey," she said.

glancing over Casey's shoulder. "There's Jake." Stephanie waved and walked down the path to meet him.

Casey had to chuckle. Even though Stephanie was joking about herself, there was some truth in all this talk of changing her personality. Stephanie had definitely become much more agreeable.

Casey was glad she could joke with Stephanie, especially about Zach. She'd been curious, and worried, about all of her sudden infatuations with cute guys. But after a day with Zach, Casey was as committed to Charley as ever.

Zach was gorgeous and worldly and entertaining. But Charley was all those things, and he was also sincere. Charley really knew Casey, and he cared about her, too.

Love is forever, Casey reminded herself, as Stephanie and Jake came over to her. And Charley was definitely her love.

Pam pushed open the door of the alliance center and stepped into the almost deserted lobby. All of the makeshift dressing rooms had been taken down, and even the posters advertising the Natural Shades contest were gone from the bulletin boards. But there was still some contest debris around.

Pam walked down the hall and poked her head into the room where she'd had her picture taken. Richard was packing up the lights, and Jesse and a few other Natural Shades reps were filing away bios and head shots. They were stacking them in cardboard boxes that had the words Wilder University scrawled on the sides in black marker.

Pam knocked on the open door and smiled tentatively when Jesse and the others at his table looked up.

"Hello," Pam said, waving at Jesse. "I'm sorry to interrupt. Can I talk to you for a minute?"

"Sure," Jesse replied. He whispered something to one of the other reps and then stepped out into the hall.

"This is a nice surprise," Jesse said, smiling. Then he paused and glanced over Pam's shoulder up and down the hallway. "I'm not in any danger, am I?" he teased. "Is Jamal lurking around the corner?"

"No," she said, blushing with embarrassment. "That's really why I came this morning. I'm glad I caught you before you left."

"You just made it." Jesse nodded. "We'll be out of here in an hour. Wilder was our last Midwest stop. Tomorrow we'll be in L.A., starting the West Coast search, and then we'll scout the East Coast before we come back to Chicago."

"So your job is not just fun and games, huh?" Pam joked.

"Nope," Jesse agreed. "You wouldn't believe how exhausting it can be searching for gorgeous women," he teased. "But seriously, it's great to see you."

"Thanks," Pam said. "I really wanted to come

by to tell you how sorry I am about Jamal's behavior yesterday. And I guess I should apologize for the day before while I'm at it." She grimaced. "I just hope you and the other Natural Shades reps won't hold it against me."

"Don't worry," Jesse assured her. "It takes more than a jealous boyfriend to turn me against a beautiful woman. But I won't deny I find you very attractive," he added. "And I *was* going to ask you on a date the first time we met, but then . . ."

"Jamal," Pam said.

"I didn't press it once I knew you had a boyfriend," Jesse said. "But if being here now means you aren't that tight with him . . .?" Jesse let the question hang and took a step closer.

"No." Pam smiled sweetly. "Jamal may be a bit rough around the edges, but he's still my guy."

"Ah, well." Jesse shrugged good-naturedly. "Can't blame a guy for trying."

"Thanks for the thought." Pam put her hand on his arm. "I'm *really* flattered. Especially since I know how many beautiful women you see."

"I have a good eye." Jesse winked at her.

Pam blushed and stepped away. "Well, if I *do* get the modeling job," she added, flashing a silly grin, "I hope we can be friends."

"Of course." Jesse smiled. "And by the way, you do have a very good chance of being selected as one of our models."

He held up his hand and crossed two fingers. "Good luck," he said. "I'm hoping we'll see each other again."

"Thanks. Me, too," Pam said excitedly. She held up her own crossed fingers, on both hands, and Jesse laughed.

"I'm glad you guys are here," Nancy said when she spotted Casey, Stephanie, and Jake standing near the elevator in the Thayer Hall lobby. "Has anyone seen Zach?" she asked breathlessly as she and Anna sprinted over to them.

"I was sure you'd be looking for *me*," Jake said, pouting. "I'm the one you have a date with this afternoon."

Nancy smiled and squeezed his arm. "I didn't forget," she said, "but we've got to find Zach first."

"He was here a minute ago," Stephanie said.

"Where did he go!" Anna cried, bouncing nervously on the balls of her feet.

Nancy noticed Casey turn to smile at Anna, but when she saw Anna's face, Casey did a double take.

"Aren't you Zach's sister?" Casey asked.

"What?" Anna replied.

"His sister?" Nancy repeated, looking from Anna to the puzzled expression on Casey's face. "She's not Zach's sister," Nancy explained. "This is Anna Pederson, my Helping Hands Little Sister."

"Oh," Casey said, shaking her head and shrugging. "That's weird. You look exactly like Zach's sister."

"And how would you know?" Stephanie asked. "Don't tell me your day at Adventure World included a quick trip home to meet Zach's family."

"No," Casey replied, "but Zach had a picture of you in his wallet," she said to Anna. "I mean, I thought it was you, but I guess I'm wrong."

"No," Nancy said slowly, realization washing over her. "I don't think you are." Nancy turned to Anna. "Did your father carry a picture of you in his wallet?" she asked, holding her breath.

"Sure," Anna replied. "A school picture. We just had them taken last month."

"That's it," Nancy said to Casey. "You did see a picture of Anna. In Mr. Pederson's wallet. Whoever was in the car with him took his wallet. That means it was Zach in your dad's car!" she exclaimed, grabbing Anna's shoulder.

"Zach had Mr. Pederson's wallet?" Casey asked.

"Are you saying Zach's the guy Ryan saw in the parking lot?" Jake said, acting as surprised as Nancy felt when she first thought it.

"Will someone start making sense?" Stephanie muttered, pulling out another cigarette. "You're giving me a headache."

"Where did you get those!" Nancy cried,

pouncing on the matches Stephanie took from her pocket.

"What, these?" Stephanie asked, holding out the black matchbook with *The Back Porch* printed on it in neon orange. "Zach gave them to me as a going-away gift." She shrugged. "What's the big deal? I thought it was a pretty cheap gift myself."

"Maybe just a stupid one," Nancy said soberly. "Because now I'm sure I know who was driving the car that hit Bess and Paul."

CHAPTER 13

Ginny took a deep breath as she stood before the door to Ray's dorm room. They hadn't spoken to each other since their argument on Friday night after the candlelight vigil for Paul. But Ginny had done a lot of thinking since then, especially after her talk with Frank Chung. She wondered if Ray had been thinking about her.

Finally Ginny rapped on the door. As soon as Ray opened it, she realized she'd been hoping they could work things out between them. There was the same exciting rush of emotion when she saw him, and the memory of all the good times they'd had together.

But when she saw Ray's expression, full of the confusion and pain that she'd also been feeling, Ginny knew there was no way back to the happy-go-lucky relationship they'd had before. Things had changed between them.

"Hi," Ginny said tentatively. She had to stop herself from throwing her arms around him, because that wouldn't be enough now.

Ray nodded and stepped back. "Come on in."

His invitation was so polite and formal that Ginny's heart constricted in her chest. She felt a distance between them now. And she was afraid that after she said what she'd come to say, that distance would only get wider.

"We should talk," she began as she walked into Ray's room. Usually she flopped down on his bed. But this time she walked over to his desk, pulled out the chair, and sat down.

"I guess we should," Ray said, running a hand though his short black hair.

"Ray," she began tentatively, "I'm proud of how hard you've worked to make the Beat Poets happen. And I know how much this record deal means to you."

She paused and caught his eye. The tension and worry were there, etched on his brow. Ginny wanted to help him, say something to make things easier. But she couldn't always be making life easier for him. She needed him to be there for her, too.

Ginny took a deep breath. "Ray, the last thing I want to do is get in the way of your dreams."

Ray closed his eyes and shook his head. "I was

hoping you'd be a part of that dream," he said, lifting his eyes to hers.

"Maybe that's the problem," Ginny replied. "I do want to be part of it. But it's *your* dream, Ray, not mine. You haven't bothered to ask me what my dream is," Ginny continued.

"But I thought the music was your dream, too," Ray pressed, his eyes beseeching her. "You love writing lyrics to my songs. And you have a creative gift, Ginny. Doesn't the music mean anything to you?"

"Of course the music means something to me," Ginny said. "But there *are* other ways to be creative, even in medicine."

"Medicine, Ginny? You've got to live your own life, not—" Ray started to say.

Ginny held up a hand to stop him.

"Not anyone else's idea of my life, right?" Ginny finished. "You mean my parents. But this is *my* choice, Ray, and you have to believe me. I've done a lot of thinking about this. I don't want to keep you from a successful future," Ginny went on. "But I don't want to feel that you're holding *me* back, either. You want me to support your life choices, but you're not supporting mine."

"It doesn't sound like we're going in the same direction anymore, does it?" Ray asked.

"No, I guess it doesn't," Ginny answered. "You know, ever since you mentioned leaving school, I've been afraid to think of my life without you. But maybe that's what we both need right now."

Silently Ray nodded his agreement.

Ginny felt her insides turn over. She realized that she'd been secretly hoping that Ray would disagree. That he'd say, "No way can I be apart from you, Ginny." And that they'd find a way to work this out. But now she knew that wasn't possible. The distance between them was too great.

"I'll always be here for you," Ginny said as she stood and made her way to the door.

"I hope so," Ray said, his voice low and raspy. He opened the door, and Ginny started out. But Ray put his arm out and stopped her. He turned her face to his, raised his fingers to her cheek, and softly brushed her long black hair away from her shoulder. Then he let his hand fall to his side.

Ginny's eyes locked with his, and her breath caught in her throat. She started to lean forward to kiss him but stopped. She turned away quickly, before Ray could see the tears in her eyes.

There was still a possibility of a future together, Ginny reminded herself, stepping into the hall. But somehow the sound of the door shutting behind her seemed symbolic.

Ginny didn't want to admit it yet, but this felt like the end.

"I still don't see how you can prove that Zach was in the car with Mr. Pederson," Jake said thoughtfully after Nancy had explained the situation to them.

"I think Ryan could identify Zach," Nancy said.

"And Zach might still have my dad's wallet," Anna added.

"That would make him either really careless or really stupid," Jake said.

"But he's already been both," Nancy replied. "He still had the wallet with him yesterday when he went to Adventure World with Casey, right? So why wouldn't he have it today?"

"I guess you're right," Jake agreed. "But it seems crazy."

"He pulled it out right in front of me," Casey reminded them. "Like it was no big deal. I even said something about the picture in it."

"Can we prove that Zach was driving the car?" Jake said.

"We can if his fingerprints are found on the steering wheel. I'll bet they're all over the driver's side of the car," Nancy replied.

True, Jake thought. If it turned out that Zach was in Mr. Pederson's car and that he was driving, then he was facing a lot more trouble than just a theft charge. There was leaving the scene of an accident, *and* vehicular manslaughter.

"Maybe he thought no one could trace him to the car?" Nancy wondered. "Anyway, even if Zach doesn't have the wallet now, Casey certainly saw him with it. Come on, let's get my car and find Ryan. Maybe he'll be able to identify Zach."

"I guess I should take this upstairs," Stephanie murmured, looking at Zach's bag distastefully.

"No, wait," Nancy said. "Let's take it with us. It's one more thing for Ryan to look at. He did say the guy in the parking lot was carrying a bag."

"Where are we going to find him?" Jake asked. "He might not be at Hewlitt yet. We'll have to get an address or phone number for him."

"You're right," Nancy agreed. "And besides, Ryan's not the one who's about to leave town. Maybe we should talk to Zach first," she suggested.

"Where did he say he was going?" Jake asked, turning to Casey and Stephanie.

"He's at the Underground," Casey replied, "with Bill and Dawn."

"Come on, then," Jake said. Nancy took the matchbook from Stephanie, Jake picked up Zach's duffel bag, and they headed toward the door.

"Everything looks good, Bess," Dr. Levy said, snapping her chart closed and clipping it to the foot of her bed. "You'll be out of here in a day or so."

"That's great," Bess murmured to the doctor's retreating back as he left the room. Exactly what

I want to hear. The phone rang, and Bess reached for it slowly. "Hello."

"Bess Marvin?" the voice said. "This is Jeanne Glasseburg."

"Oh," Bess replied, surprised. "Hello."

"I heard about your accident," Ms. Glasseburg said. "I hope you're okay."

"I've just gotten a thumbs-up from my doctor," Bess said. "Thanks."

"I'm glad to hear that, Bess," Ms. Glasseburg went on. "I'm sorry you didn't get to perform the other night. I was looking forward to seeing you."

"I wish I could have been there," Bess replied.

"I have been impressed with your work," Ms. Glasseburg continued. "And I've thought this situation over. Normally I wouldn't make an exception for anyone, but it didn't seem fair for you to be overlooked, considering your accident. I'm calling to tell you I'd like you to audition for my class. When you recover, of course."

"Really?" Bess asked. "Thanks."

"You can thank your friends Casey Fontaine and Brian Daglian," Ms. Glasseburg replied. "They're the ones who told me what happened to you. But it's your *talent* that's getting you the audition," she added.

Bess hung up the phone and gazed around the room. She kept waiting for the excitement and anticipation to kick in. If there was anything she might have looked forward to, the invitational class was it. She should have been giddy with happiness that Jeanne Glasseburg herself had called and offered her another chance. But she felt nothing. Bess was numb.

It was no good, she realized. She had to get out of Wilder. Nothing here could take away the empty feeling she'd had since she lost Paul.

Nancy pushed open the door to the Underground. Next to her, Jake adjusted Zach's bag on his shoulder.

"Which one is he?" Anna asked, right behind them. "Do you want me to call the police yet?"

"Hold on, tiger," Jake said, putting a hand on Anna's arm.

Nancy's eyes swept the room, taking in the small groups of people gathered around the tables with red-checked cloths. She spotted Bill, Dawn, and Zach in a far corner and started toward them.

She was only halfway across the room when they saw her. She watched Zach's eyes flick from her face to his bag on Jake's shoulder.

"Hello." Bill smiled as Nancy, Jake, and Anna drew near. "We're glad you came to join the goodbye lunch," he teased, "but you didn't have to lug Zach's bag all the way over here, Jake."

"He wasn't doing Zach a favor," Nancy said.

Zach frowned, and his eyes grew dark.

"Nancy?" Dawn asked, clearly puzzled by her tone of voice. "What's wrong?"

"I'll take that," Zach said, reaching out for his bag and smiling tightly. "Thanks."

"Do you mind if we keep it for a while?" Nancy asked. "We'd like to show it to someone. And we'd like you to come with us."

"Show it to whom?" Zach asked.

"Someone who was at Blake's Place on Thursday night," Nancy explained, her gaze shifting to Bill and Dawn for a second. "Remember, Zach? The night you got into town? This person witnessed a man helping Mr. Pederson into his car. The man was carrying a bag, and we want to know if it was this one."

"Nancy?" Bill said, suddenly catching on to the conversation. "Are you saying Zach had something to do with that accident?"

Nancy reached into her pocket and pulled out the matchbook she'd taken from Stephanie. She tossed it onto the table, and Bill picked it up.

"What are these for?" he asked.

"These are the matches Zach just gave to Stephanie," Nancy explained. "The person who was at Blake's Place found some on the bar there Thursday night. And another book of the same matches was found in Mr. Pederson's car after the accident."

"So what's the crime?" Zach blurted out, trying to laugh. "I know there's a big antismoking campaign going on, but smoking is still legal. Lots of people carry around matches from bars."

"Except that this bar happens to be in Los

168

Angeles," Nancy replied grimly. "Which you could have passed through on your travels. Not too many other people in Weston had been to L.A. lately."

Zach looked startled and opened his mouth, but he had nothing to say.

"You've been pretty careless with these matchbooks, Zach," Nancy added. "Leaving them all over town, in Blake's Place"—she paused—"and in Mr. Pederson's car."

"Look," Zach said, clearing his throat nervously, "I don't know what you're talking about. Mr. Pederson? I didn't leave any matches in his car."

"It wasn't just the matches, Zach," Nancy continued. "Didn't you tell Bill you'd lost your sunglasses?"

Zach didn't reply, but Bill nodded.

"Zach always wears sunglasses," Bill said. "He told me he just misplaced a pair."

"There was an extra pair of sunglasses in Mr. Pederson's car," Nancy said. "Oval-shaped, with wire frames. Very hip."

"That's the type," Bill muttered.

"And they weren't my dad's!" Anna cried out, glaring at Zach angrily.

"You got in late Thursday night," Nancy continued. "You stopped at Blake's Place with your duffel, had a few drinks, and tried to hitch a ride. But Mr. Pederson was too drunk to drive, Zach, so you took the wheel."

"No!" Zach said, standing up quickly, his chair clattering to the floor.

"Mr. Pederson also said his wallet was missing," Nancy said. "He had a picture of Anna in it. Doesn't she look familiar, Zach?" Nancy pressed. "Don't tell me you've already forgotten the 'sister' whose picture you carry in your wallet. Or is that *your* wallet?"

Zach looked at Anna carefully. His eyes lit with recognition. Then his face drained of color.

"But since you weren't in the car," Jake added, "I guess you won't mind if we check your bag for the wallet."

Immediately Zach's hands went to his pockets. But then he realized what he'd done, and his face flushed. "I've got to get g-going," Zach stuttered, looking at Bill helplessly.

"Zach? Tell me this isn't true, man," Bill begged.

Zach took a step back.

Jake blocked him, and in an instant Bill was on his feet, gripping Zach's arm.

"You're not going anywhere," Bill said sadly, disappointment all over his face.

"You've got a lot of explaining to do," Nancy added. "And I think it's finally time to call the police," she said, gazing down at Anna's face.

CHAPTER 14

It was hard to believe that things could be so calm, but Suite 301 in the middle of the week was dead silent, and Dawn finally had some time alone—no middle-of-the-night tragedy, no freshman crisis.

And no Bill. She sighed.

Dawn hadn't seen him since Sunday, when Nancy, Jake, and Anna had come into the Underground airing their suspicions about Zach being the hit-and-run driver in Bess and Paul's accident.

They'd turned out to be right about Zach, and Dawn knew Bill must have had a tough few days. She'd wanted to see him, but she had her own responsibilities and hadn't had a moment free—until now.

Well, you certainly aren't going to see him sitting here, she told herself. Dawn pulled herself off the couch, locked the suite door behind her, and loped down the stairs two at a time.

Bill answered the door on her second knock. Right away, Dawn could see how upset he was.

"Is this a good time? I've been wanting to see you," Dawn said, coming into the room, "to find out what happened with Zach."

Bill flinched when he heard Zach's name. "For starters, he's in jail on a vehicular manslaughter charge."

"So he really was driving," Dawn said.

Bill nodded. "Nancy was right about everything," he replied. "Zach stopped at Blake's Place that night for a quick drink before coming here. He needed a ride to campus, so he tried to hitch one from Mr. Pederson. But the guy was so drunk, Zach decided to drive and took the keys from him."

"It's kind of ironic, isn't it?" Dawn said.

Bill looked puzzled.

"Well, at first Zach was doing the right thing, you know? He was trying to keep the guy from driving, so he wouldn't get in an accident and kill somebody." Dawn said.

"But he stopped doing the right thing as soon as he got in the car," Bill replied. "He'd run out of money, and he was broke. That's why he came back to the U.S. in the first place. Anyway, Zach figured he'd lift the guy's wallet to get some extra cash."

"Oh." Dawn cringed.

"He was driving fast," Bill went on. "And he took his eyes off the road for a second to check Mr. Pederson's pockets for the wallet. When he looked up, he was speeding through the intersection, and he was practically on top of the motorcycle before he saw it."

Dawn groaned, covering her mouth.

"It was too late to brake or swerve. He'd clipped the back of the bike already, and he barely kept the car from spinning off the road," Bill finished, his voice cool. "Zach panicked and took off. He parked the car on some side street and just left the guy in there, passed out cold."

"And he *still* kept the wallet?" Dawn asked.

"Can you believe it?" Bill asked. "He had no idea what had happened to the people on the motorcycle, and he probably didn't care. What he did care about was the money. Pretty harsh, huh?"

Dawn could only nod.

"Zach had a bunch of matchbooks from the Back Porch, a surfer hangout in Los Angeles," Bill explained, "and I don't think he realized he was leaving them all over town. And he'd dropped his sunglasses in Mr. Pederson's car," he said, glancing at her, "not on some exotic beach."

"This must be hard for you," Dawn said sympathetically. She could see the hurt and anger on Bill's face.

"Zach was a good friend. I always knew he was a little wild," Bill said. "But I never realized he was cold and heartless. I can't believe he actually killed someone—and didn't even care."

Bill closed his eyes for a moment, then looked at her. "I wish Zach had never contacted me," Bill whispered angrily.

"Bill," Dawn said, moving toward him, "none of this was your fault. He may have been coming to see you, but his actions are his own."

Bill shrugged. "Whatever," he said, his voice cheerless. "I'd rather not have any more visitors for a while."

"Good." Dawn nodded. "That's a great idea."

She noticed that Bill heard the different tone in her voice. He looked up with a puzzled frown.

"Because I've wanted to get you to myself for a while," Dawn explained, stepping closer to him and slipping her arm around his shoulders.

"You have?" Bill asked.

"I've wanted to talk to you about our relationship," Dawn answered, stroking the back of his neck lightly. "It's taken me a while to know what's really in my heart."

Dawn saw the change in Bill's expression, the tiny flicker of hope and longing in his eyes.

"Does that mean . . ." he began. "Are you saying what I think you're saying?"

Dawn nodded. "I want us to be more than just good friends."

Tentatively Bill circled her waist with his arms. Then he pressed his palm against her back and Dawn shivered. The glint in Bill's eye told her he felt it.

"You're sure?" he asked, his voice husky.

Dawn's answer was a long, sweet kiss.

"We've packed all of your sweaters," Nancy said, zipping one of Bess's suitcases closed. "What's left?"

"T-shirt drawer, I guess," Bess said as she watched Nancy, George, and Leslie, her roommate, go through her dresser and closet. She was finally out of the hospital and back at Jamison Hall. Her parents would arrive in less than an hour to drive her home to River Heights.

Right now everyone thought she was only going home for a short time, just to recuperate. Unless Bess wanted an argument, she couldn't admit that this was definitely good-bye.

Not only were Nancy, George, and Leslie packing her stuff, but Jake and Will were waiting to help her carry it downstairs. Casey and Brian were trying to keep everyone entertained.

"You are going to audition for Glasseburg when you come back, right?" Casey asked for the hundredth time.

Bess nodded and summoned a smile. She knew what her friends had done on her behalf, and she appreciated it, but she couldn't promise anything just now.

"You probably won't believe this, Bess," Leslie said, "but I don't know what I'm going to do without you."

"You'll be able to get some studying done, for a change," Bess replied.

"Maybe, but I really will miss you," Leslie said.

"I know." Bess smiled. "Thanks."

Bess glanced over and saw Will leaning in her doorway, his face drawn. She walked over to him, knowing there was one thing she had to do before she left.

"Listen," Bess said, pulling Will into the hall for a minute. "Can I talk to you?"

Bess put her good hand on Will's arm. "George told me that you've been feeling guilty for lending us the motorcycle," she said bluntly.

"I'm sorry," Will blurted out, looking miserable. "I wish I could take it back—"

"Please don't say that," Bess interrupted, her voice thick with emotion. "The accident wasn't your fault just because we were riding your motorcycle. Any more than it was Mr. Pederson's fault because his car was involved."

"But if you'd been in a car," Will said, "Paul might still be alive."

"If we hadn't gone at all, he'd still be alive," Bess replied. "It was my idea to have a picnic, and Nancy suggested that we go to the state park.

Don't you see, Will? We can *all* blame ourselves if we want to."

"I know," Will groaned, "but that doesn't make me feel any less guilty."

"Will," Bess said urgently, "the accident was Zach's fault and no one else's. I'll miss Paul for the rest of my life, and I don't know how I'll get over it," she continued. "But our last day together was the most beautiful day of my life," Bess admitted, tears filling her eyes. "It was perfect. We *loved* riding around on your bike, and that's the way I'll always remember him."

"Thank you," Will whispered, dropping his head onto her shoulder and holding her tightly in his arms. "It means a lot to me to hear you say that."

"Now wipe your eyes, come inside, and help me take my stuff down to the car," Bess ordered with a weak grin.

Just then Eileen and Holly came running down the hall with a big plastic garbage bag.

"I'm glad we caught you," Eileen cried, breathing heavily.

"We wanted to bring you these," Holly said, holding out the bag.

Bess peeked into the bag and saw a pile of candy bars. "What do you want to do, make me fat?" Bess wailed.

"We just want you to indulge yourself a little," Eileen said. "We're happy that you're still with us, that's all," she said, blinking quickly to keep from crying.

"Thanks," Bess said softly.

"We're all going to miss you," Holly promised.

"Even Soozie?" Bess teased.

"Believe it or not, she was truly upset when she heard about what happened," Holly said. She gave Bess a quick hug. "Come back soon. Kappa's no fun without you."

Bess forced a smile onto her own face, before anxiously checking her watch. Her parents would be downstairs in a few minutes, and she couldn't wait to leave.

Her life on campus was too painful. There were memories of Paul everywhere Bess looked. She gazed around at all her friends and felt a pang of guilt. She was grateful for the way they were trying to cheer her up. And she knew they really cared.

If only they knew how desperate I am to get away from here, Bess thought, clenching her teeth and trying to ignore the pain in her heart.

"Hey, is that the Natural Babe?"

Pam was on her way into the Student Union when she looked up and spotted Reva Ross waving at her from the front door.

"Oh, darling," Pam joked. "No autographs. I'm traveling naturally collegiate today. You know, trying to pass as a normal college student."

"Andy loved the test photos they gave me,"

Reva said. "But he swore he'd buy every copy of every magazine I was ever in if I won. It's so sweet the way he doesn't want to share me with the world." Reva laughed.

"Jamal doesn't even want to hear about it." Pam grimaced. "He thinks I'm too smart for that kind of thing."

"I see," Reva said thoughtfully. "I'm sure he's right, then. The contest was probably a waste of time."

"Pretty silly even to enter," Pam agreed.

The girls looked at each other and then burst out laughing.

"Who are we kidding?" Reva said. "I'd do it again in a second."

"Me, too," Pam agreed. She remembered the giddy feeling of being sent in for photographs, and the picture of herself that Jesse had shown her.

"Why should we pass up a chance at fame and fortune just because we're pretty *and* smart?" Reva asked.

"Of course my chance of *winning* is a total long shot," Pam admitted, flashing a sneaky grin. "But I can still hope."

"I can, too," Reva said.

It did seem pretty farfetched to entertain hopes of winning the Natural Shades contest. The chances were as slim as the odds of walking to the nearest drugstore, buying a lottery ticket, and winning ten million dollars.

But even so, Pam knew she'd be on pins and needles until she found out who had been chosen.

"Packing up her stuff was pretty tough, wasn't it?" Jake asked Nancy as they walked back to Thayer after saying goodbye to Bess.

"It was," Nancy admitted. "I just hope Bess comes through this all right."

"She will," Jake said, putting his arm around Nancy's waist and pulling her close. "She's got you and George for best friends.

"But this kind of grief is something I've had no experience with," Nancy said. "I was very young when my mother died, and I don't know if I can really understand what Bess is going through."

"Maybe not," Jake said. "We all grieve in our own way. But at least Bess knows she can count on you, and that's what will matter the most."

"I'm glad we have a break coming up," Nancy said. "It'll be nice to see Bess so soon. I'm sure she'll need some company."

"This trip to River Heights means a lot to me, too," Jake commented, taking Nancy's hand in his. "I'm really looking forward to it."

"Meeting my dad and seeing my old stomping ground?" Nancy grinned.

"Sure," Jake replied. "And your room and all the cute pictures of you when you were little."

"No way," Nancy protested. "No baby pictures."

"Come on," Jake begged. "You're beautiful."

"Thank you, but I was weird-looking as a kid," Nancy said, laughing. "I don't need to relive my childhood. She noticed someone familiar standing near the brightly lit doorway to Thayer.

"Wait a minute. Is that Anna?" Nancy asked. "Hey there!" she cried, waving her arms over her head. "I wonder what she's doing on campus so late," Nancy said as she and Jake hurried to the doorway.

"Hi, Nancy," Anna said. Then she looked at Jake and smiled shyly. "Hello," she added softly.

"What's up?" Nancy asked. "Is everything okay at home?"

"Yes," Anna said. "Thanks to you."

Looking down at Anna's grinning face, Nancy felt a warm rush of pleasure.

"What are you doing here so late?" Nancy asked.

"It's about my dad," Anna admitted, pausing a minute. "I have good news and bad news."

"Oh, no," Nancy said, frowning. "Give me the good news first."

"The good news is that he hasn't had a drink since the accident." Anna smiled. "*And* he found a job!"

"Congratulations!" Nancy grinned. She bent down to give Anna a hug.

"What's the bad news?" Jake blurted out.

"His new job isn't in Weston," Anna said, bitting her lip.

181

"You're leaving town?" Nancy asked sadly, a wave of disappointment rushing over her.

Anna nodded.

"I'm glad for your dad," Nancy said, "but I'll miss you."

"I'll miss you, too," Anna replied, blushing. "But we still have to find a house, so we won't be leaving Weston right away."

"Well, you'd better let me take you out for a special goodbye dinner," Nancy added.

"I promise," Anna said. "I'll call you soon," she yelled back as she started down the hill toward town. "Thanks again, Nancy. You're the greatest!"

"I have to agree," Jake whispered in her ear, as they watched Anna disappear toward town.

"With what?" Nancy asked.

"About your being the greatest," Jake explained, pulling her close.

Slowly Jake turned Nancy around so that she was facing him.

"Are you sure you want me to go home with you over the break?" Jake asked. "I really want to meet your family, but I don't want to rush you. I want everything to feel good."

"I'm sure," Nancy said. "I'm feeling good about a lot of things right now," she added, wrapping her arms around him. And one of the most important things, Nancy knew, was not letting the past hold her back.

Her talk with Ned the day before had been

wonderful, not only because it helped remind Nancy of what they had meant to each other in the past, but also because it told her what they were now—just friends.

It was all right to move on. And taking Jake home to River Heights to meet her father was just the beginning. Nancy was looking forward to the coming break more than ever.

"You're the greatest," Nancy whispered happily as she gazed into Jake's warm brown eyes and waited eagerly for his lips to meet hers.

NEXT iN NANCY DREW ON CAMPUS™:

Exams are finally over, and Nancy and George have big plans for the long weekend. They're heading home to River Heights, not only to check on Bess, who's in the hospital recuperating from her accident, but to spend time with Jake and Will—which means introducing the guys to their families. And they thought all the tests were done! But Nancy has plenty to keep her busy—like the hot new audiotapes Jake's found. Too hot, in fact: They're counterfeit copies, and someone could end up paying a high price if caught selling them. Meanwhile, back on campus, Stephanie's wondering if the new guy in her life is offering true romance or counterfeit affection—which also can exact a painfully high price . . . in *Going Home,* Nancy Drew on Campus #16.